BOSS
OF THE
NAMKO
DRIVE

BOSS OF THE NAMKO DRIVE

PAUL ST. PIERRE

Douglas & McIntyre
Vancouver/Toronto

Douglas & McIntyre Ltd., 1615 Venables Street, Vancouver, British Columbia V5L 2H1

Canadian Cataloguing in Publication Data
   St. Pierre, Paul, 1923–
      Boss of the Namko drive

      ISBN 0-88894-494-2

      I. Title.
PS8537.A54B67 1986   jC813'.54   C85-091595-3
PZ7.S183Bo 1986

Cover photograph by Stephen Bosch
Printed and bound in Canada by D.W. Friesen & Sons

This book is dedicated to my children,
PAUL, MICHELLE and SUZANNE,
who did part of their growing up in Chilcotin.

PREFACE

Young people for whom this story is written should not try to find Namko on the map of British Columbia. They might guess where it is, and some have, but it is not on the maps. In the same way, the characters in the book are fictional.

There is, of course, such a region as I describe. It is called Chilcotin, or, in the local style of speaking, The Chilcotin Country. It is the farthest west and the farthest north extension of the North American cattle ranges, a high and handsome plateau which lies between the Fraser River and the Coast Mountains in British Columbia. There are still beef drives up there, but in the 1980s they are short drives of small bunches of cattle from spring to summer ranges or from summer range to home ranches. The long drives to market, such as were carried out when this book was written, have now ended.

However, the style of life depicted here has not ended and will not end in my lifetime or in yours. There will always be ranch lands, they will always be on the edges of the richer ground, and they will always nourish children who are, by nature and training, survivors.

Without blaming them for errors in this book, I would like to express my thanks to the following people for their constructive criticism of the original *Boss* manuscript: Gene Mooney, his wife, Carol, and his son Montgomery, who then ranched at Anahim Lake, B.C.; the late Gabriel Lane-Bayliff of Chilahnko Ranch at Alexis Creek, B.C.; Buck Kindt, who cowboyed many years ago in the Peace River Country, and the late Alan Morley, newspaperman and author. *Boss of the Namko Drive* first appeared in the "Cariboo Country" CBC television series.

28 August 1985
Fort Langley, B.C.

CONTENTS

THE GREEN MOUNTAIN MORGAN

The beef drive was ready to move out at first light. It was the only thing that ever started on time in the Namko country.

Delore counted one hundred and ninety-seven animals on the three-mile-long meadow called the Long Opening. The usual stock. Herefords, more or less. A little Shorthorn and Angus blood ran in most of them. Ranchers in the Namko range claimed that pure Hereford became too rangy, too long in the leg. Delore had heard his mother say that this was just an excuse for indifferent breeding, but the visiting ranchers and cowboys did not argue this point with her, they just passed over her opinion.

One hundred and ninety-seven. The year's increase from a dozen small ranches which were spread over fifteen hundred square miles of the farthest west cattle range in Canada. Frenchie Bernard, Delore's father, sometimes said, "We have got the only ranch between Larsen's Three Circle place and Mongolia."

Delore shifted his right hip against the cantle of the stock saddle and crossed his forearms over the leather-bound roping horn. One hundred and ninety-seven. That was just about exactly the number of miles they

had to push this drive from Namko to the Pacific Great
Eastern Railway's stockyard at Williams Lake. Most
people said it was a two-hundred-mile drive and the
longest in North America, but nobody was certain.
Maps were not that accurate.

Delore had tried to determine the distance the night
before. There had been many other jobs to do first.
He had checked all his saddle rigging. He had carefully inspected the feet of his little buckskin mare,
Stella. He fluffed up his old army-surplus sleeping bag,
which was more chicken feather than eiderdown, and
wished for a better one. He honed his knife and packed
some extra socks and a sweater into one of the boxes
that the packhorses would carry. Only then, long
after his father and mother and younger brothers had
gone to bed, only then did Delore sit down beside the
hissing gas lantern and try to trace the Beef Trail on the
four - mile - to - the - inch map issued by the British
Columbia Department of Agriculture. For most of the
area, it was the best map to be had. There was not yet
a mile-to-the-inch map of this part of British Columbia.
The map showed a dotted line where Lieutenant
Palmer of the Royal Engineers had crossed the Chilcotin Plateau in 1863. Lieutenant Palmer had paral-
lelled much of the route of Sir Alexander Mackenzie
who, in 1793, had made the first known white man's
journey overland to the Pacific Ocean north of Mexico.

Perhaps Alexander Mackenzie had walked across this
very meadow, following the slope of the land toward
the Coast Range where the sun sparkled now on the
mountain snow crust. Most books gave the impression
that Mackenzie had crossed the country by canoe, but

people in the Namko country knew that nobody could fiddle around in these little creeks by canoe.

Delore found it hard to imagine that a man could walk two hundred miles. For as long as he could remember he had travelled by saddle horse. He was given a horse of his own at the age of eight and now, at fifteen, he owned the fast little mare, Stella. He only wished he could stay on her back all the way to Williams Lake. Probably, during the three-week drive, he would have to give her a few days' rest while he rode one of those knotheads that made up the pack train.

Stella turned her head. Delore looked, too. One of the old cows in the drive had begun to move off toward the pines at the edge of the meadow, taking four fat steers with her. Clearly she intended to go back to her home ranch. She had, as cowboys said, looked over the situation here, considered it all very carefully and decided she did not want any part of it. Delore clenched his legs, just slightly. That was all that Stella needed. He never used the spurs on her now. He laid the rein gently across the left side of her neck, low, at the same time his legs told her to run. In an instant they were at a full gallop, moving to cut off the knot of Herefords before they lost themselves in the timber. The reins to her bit were long. Delore held them lightly in his left hand. His right hand held the three feet of trailing reins and he whirled this in a circle, making a dull buzzing sound, and shouted, "Hi yi, yi, yi!" The Herefords turned back toward the meadow.

Delore and Stella came up close behind them and Delore slapped the ends of the reins against his chaps.

He kept yipping. The cow and steers broke into an awkward gallop that made him laugh. It was almost as much fun as chasing moose away from the haystacks in winter. Moose trotted beautifully, but if you scared them enough to gallop they looked ridiculous. Step-and-a-Half, the old cowboy, used to say that moose galloped as though they had been taught how to do it in correspondence school.

"Ay!" shouted Frenchie. "Delore! Have some sense."

Frenchie was white-haired. He had a long, thin nose and three gold teeth. Two fingers were missing from his right hand but he never told anybody why. As far as Delore knew, even his mother did not know. She told him once that she had asked his father but Frenchie had only grunted. It was a great deal easier to talk with his mother than with his father. Perhaps for this reason he always called his mother "Mother," but he called his father "Frenchie." So did everybody else in Namko, the cowboys, the Indians and the other ranchers.

Once his father won a bet with another rancher named Ken Larsen by signing a cheque *Frenchie Bernard* in that awkward handwriting of his and getting it cashed at the Royal Bank in Williams Lake. The banker had laughed and said, "Well, I guess there is only one Frenchie Bernard in the Cariboo country." His father had just grunted, and after they came out on the street and walked down the board sidewalk toward the Maple Leaf Hotel his father had told him that he did not like bankers. To Delore that seemed unfair, because the banker had been friendly. But he said nothing.

There was something about his father that frightened

him, but he did not know what it was. Frenchie never hit him or any of his younger brothers, except just once when Delore had called Ol Antoine "a dirty old Siwash." Frenchie had hit him then, not on the seat of his pants as he saw some other children get bunted, but right in the mouth so that his lip bled. And that was strange, too, because Frenchie himself called Indians "Siwashes" whenever he got angry with them.

Now, as his father rode up, it was clear that he was angry. Delore sat as still as he could on the little mare. She shifted her feet beneath him. It was almost like a dance. She, too, seemed to know that Frenchie was angry.

"Do you see them cowboys tarryhootin' hafter stock dat way?" said Frenchie. Sometimes Frenchie's accent was very strong.

Delore looked over the Long Opening. Step-and-a-Half Jones was sitting his bay with his arms folded across the saddle horn. Walter Charlie was walking his horse beside a little bunch of cattle which carried Larsen's Three Circle on their rumps. And Anatole Harry, the second Indian, was pushing a couple of other animals into the big mass of the Namko drive by just saying, "Shish, shish, shish," through his two missing front teeth and slapping his hand very softly on his big, shiny black chaps.

"And they're only cowboys," said Frenchie. "Hat least they don't run the fat off the beef. They know they got to walk dem. Walk dem. Walk dem. Walk dem."

"Okay," said Delore.

"Walk dem, I say. Anybody can get a cowboy to

gallop haround like the movies. In this countree, we need cow *men*."

Frenchie walked his saddle horse away from Delore just as Anatole walked his up. Anatole and Delore sat their horses alongside one another, watching Frenchie walk his horse toward Four Mile Creek, which cut across the big meadow.

"I don't know what for he rides that saddle horse," said Anatole.

"He bought him at Williams Lake Stampede," said Delore.

"Aha," said Anatole softly. By the tone of his voice Delore realized that Anatole knew perfectly well how Frenchie got the horse.

The Morgan had been the toughest saddle bronc of all the rodeos in the Cariboo one summer. But when Frenchie had ridden him at the big Williams Lake Stampede, he would not buck. When the gate of the side delivery chute had been dragged open the Morgan would not move out. Other cowboys on the rails of the chute prodded him. Still the black horse would not move. Finally, one came up with an electric prod and the saddle bronc had made two little crow hops onto the stampede grounds, but that was all.

Frenchie was given a reride. The owner of the Morgan, embarrassed, sold the horse to Frenchie for a hundred dollars, double or nothing, price to be decided by flipping a coin. Frenchie won the toss and got the Morgan for nothing.

It was big by cow pony standards, weighing probably thirteen hundred. Frenchie claimed that it was the Green Mountain strain of Morgan, which produced, he said, the best horses known to the race of man. His mother insisted the horse had Percheron blood, a charge which made Frenchie indignant. It was coal black, heavy in the lower jowl, and always of a sultry disposition.

It had bitten his little brother, Robbie. Delore's mother was afraid of it, and he had never seen her show fear of any other horse on the ranch. Its ears lay back whenever Delore came near, and once it had lashed out suddenly with its hind feet and almost caught him full in the chest. Delore was ready to jump because he saw the Morgan's ears go back when he came close to it, so the hooves barely touched his chest as he fell backward. Frenchie said afterwards that if Delore had not been fast enough in jumping backward the Morgan's hooves would have punched in his ribs and killed him, but his father would not shoot the horse. Some people, a few months after his father won the horse, claimed that it had killed two riders, one at the Calgary Stampede and another at Oroville, Washington. His father did not believe them.

A coyote-dun saddle horse on the Larsen's Three Circle ranch had tried to stomp Mrs. Larsen once when she fell, and Ken Larsen had tied the horse, run to the house, brought out his carbine and shot the horse right where it stood. But Delore's father was different. He claimed that the Morgan was a good horse if it was not mistreated, and said that Delore must have done something to make it kick. When Delore's mother said she was afraid of the horse, too, Frenchie said very sharply that the Green Mountain Morgan was one of the best horses in all the Namko country and that there was no need for anyone to be afraid of him. So they all left the big, black saddle horse alone, except Frenchie, who could do anything with him.

Delore and Anatole watched Frenchie as he rode away on the black. Frenchie's back was stiff with anger. It infuriated him to see cattle galloped, his own or anybody else's. At a boggy section of the meadow the Morgan began to dance. It was afraid of sinking through the unnaturally green patch of grass into the deep mud that it knew lay beneath.

Frenchie clenched his legs to push the horse through the boggy section. The Morgan danced some more. Frenchie dug in his big, steel spurs. The big black broke loose underneath him. First it put its head down almost between its knees, pulling the reins out of Frenchie's hands. Frenchie had not expected this, and the reins dropped.

Any good cow pony stands still when its reins hit the ground. But the Green Mountain Morgan was not a good cow pony, as everybody except Frenchie knew. It humped its back, kicked its legs almost straight out behind it and nearly dumped Frenchie on its first jump. Frenchie had no reins to hold. He started to fall off the left side of the horse, but at the same time the Morgan began to spin to the right. It was the action rodeo riders call "sunspinning." Frenchie's weight combined with the horse's fast turn and horse and man went down together. The horse rolled almost over the top of the man. As it did, there was a *pop* that Delore could hear in the pit of his stomach. Even before he and Anatole ran their horses toward Frenchie he knew he had heard his father's leg breaking.

"NOT STEP-AND-A-HALF"

Anatole rode back to the Bernard ranch to bring Delore's mother. Delore stayed beside his father. Walter Charlie rode up. It seemed he had heard the leg bone pop even on the opposite side of the meadow. But after looking at them for a minute he said, "I guess, might be I better keep this drive in one place." Then he moved off and kept circling the edges of the meadow, pushing back cows that broke for the timber, keeping the whole one hundred and ninety-seven bawling, stupid creatures in a shifting brown-and-white patch in the centre of the Long Opening. Walter did not seem to care whether Frenchie's leg had broken or not.

While he waited for his mother Delore spoke a couple of times to his father. His father's nose looked thinner than ever, almost like a hawk's beak. The skin on his face looked like wax. His eyes were closed.

"What can I do for you, Frenchie?" said Delore.

His father whispered something through his teeth, which he kept tight together.

"I can't hear you," said Delore.

His father spoke again, through his teeth. "I said leave me alone."

There was no answer to this, so Delore sat beside

9

him in silence until his mother rode across the meadow beside Anatole, riding bareback on the old paint. She could ride almost any kind of a horse, and ride it well, saddle or no saddle.

Delore's mother had a strange accent. It was not like his father's, it was not like the Indians'. He did not know what it was, and she never told him. She was dark and graceful and had long hair that hung almost to her hips, until she bound it up in the mornings in braids and wound the braids around her head. She slipped off the paint and walked, instead of running, to where Frenchie lay on the grass. Delore noticed his mother was like the Indians: at the worst of times she could move slowly and without getting excited or loud-voiced. She carried an old potato sack in her right hand. She had used her left to hold the old rope halter on the paint as she galloped him across the grass. She spoke first to Delore.

"Is it broken, Delore?"

"I think so."

She held the bottom of the sack, gave a quick flip of her wrist, and spilled the contents on the grass. There were bandages, iodine, scissors, adhesive tape, aspirin, half a bottle of B.C. Liquor Control Board whisky, and a few other bits and pieces from the kitchen cupboard where the first-aid kit was stowed.

Delore's mother was a very gentle woman, whose voice was low and soft. But she was not this way when she knelt beside Frenchie and spilled the sack open beside his head.

"You are a fool," she said. "A fool. Everybody knew that Morgan would break your bones some day."

"Shut hup," said Frenchie. "Dere is nothin' wrong with dat Morgan."

Delore's mother passed her hand down Frenchie's leg until she came to the top of his high-heeled cowboy boot. They were new boots. Frenchie bought them the previous fall when he took a drive over the Namko trail. He had not worn them since, because in Namko most cowboys and ranchers wore high-ankle Chilcotin moccasins inside short rubbers in cold weather and ordinary boots much of the rest of the time. But Frenchie had brought the new boots out again for the long drive to the Lake.

"It's a full break," said Delore's mother.

"Hit wasn't dat 'orse's fault," said Frenchie. "He just started playin'."

"That horse has killed two men and is still trying for a third," said Delore's mother.

"No," said Frenchie. He started to sit up but the pain in his leg made him fall back again. He lay flat on the grass and looked at the sky.

"There is nothin' wrong with that horse," he said. "Just fix that leg."

"Nothing will fix this leg except time. It is broken right across the top of the ankle. I will splint it and we will take you down to the store on the hay wagon. Then the mail truck can take you in to the hospital at the Lake."

"I know hit's broke. I don't need somebody to tell me my leg is broke."

Delore's mother passed the whisky bottle to Frenchie and said, "Start drinking this. Get it inside you, because the pain is going to be very bad when we straighten it out and start to splint."

Frenchie said, "Delore must take in the drive."

"Never mind about Delore. Drink the whisky."

"Where is Delore? Delore . . .? Come here."

"Drink the whisky. If you drink it all at one time you will get sick and vomit. Drink it slowly and get it inside you. Here. Start." She held Frenchie's head and put the whisky bottle against his lips. Frenchie brushed it aside. Some of the whisky spilt on the grass. Delore's mother caught the bottle as it fell and put it in Frenchie's hand again.

"Yes, Frenchie," said Delore.

"You 'ave got to take the drive to the Lake."

Delore's mother said, "Delore is too young. Let Step-and-a-Half take the drive in."

Frenchie said, "No."

"Step can take in the drive."

"Hi said *no*," said Delore's father. Frenchie lifted himself on his elbows, then fell back, very white. White and tired as he looked, he said through his closed teeth, "Not Step. Delore will take in the drive."

"Delore is a boy. Step is a man. Let Step take the drive."

"Not Step."

"Why not Step?"

His father lay silent. Beads of sweat grew on his forehead and toppled down his cheeks.

"Walter Charlie?" said Delore's mother.

His father was silent.

"Anatole Harry?"

Silence.

"Then let Step boss the drive."

His father opened his eyes very wide and seemed to look at a large white cloud that was passing above the Long Opening. He said, "Delore will take in the Namko drive."

"Sip that whisky," said Delore's mother. "This is going to hurt." She moved down beside Frenchie's legs. She looked at the left leg. It was twisted, just where the top of the high boot reached. "A bad break," she said, "but a clean one. Delore, take your knife, cut off that boot."

Frenchie came up on his elbows again. "Don't cut that boot," he said, "it cost twenty-five dollars."

"Shut up," Mrs. Frenchie said sharply. She spoke to Delore again. "Take the knife. Cut off the boot."

Delore began to cut down from the top of the riding boot. It was a handsome boot, the best he had ever seen his father wear. This pair had not been ordered from the mail-order house, like most of the equipment at Frenchie's ranch; they had been bought in the saddle shop at Williams Lake with money Frenchie had won on some bet.

"Don't cut that boot," said Frenchie.

Delore's mother said again, very firmly, "Cut the boot."

Delore cut the boot, trying not to jar his father's leg. He still felt sick at his stomach.

After the boot was off his mother said, "Put your foot in his crotch and pull this leg straight." She had thin wood splints, cut from an apple box, to bind around Frenchie's leg.

Delore worked his own high-heeled riding boot

between his father's legs and gently into his crotch.
Then, taking the foot of the broken leg, he pulled with
all his strength. He was now quite sure that he was
going to vomit. His father made a harsh sound and
fainted.

"That's good," said his mother. "He's fainted. Now
he won't feel any pain for a while."

She laid the splints against the leg and with surprising speed began to wrap the bandage to hold them
tight against the two ends of the break, which were now
flush. After a few wraps she said, "Delore, he might
have swallowed his tongue. Go up and push this into
his mouth." She tossed him a piece of splint. She
slipped her own leg beside Delore's inside Frenchie's
two limp legs. Delore let go his grip on his father's
ankle and moved, on his knees, to his father's head.
Frenchie looked grey. His breathing was harsh, like a
snore.

"Pull open his jaws," said his mother sharply. "If he
swallows his tongue he'll strangle himself." He reluctantly put his hands into his father's mouth, pulled
down the lower jaw, fished for the wet tongue, pulled
it down and shoved in the piece of wood.

"Well back," said his mother. "Well back. Right to
the back teeth."

Delore shoved the stick far back into his father's
mouth.

"That's better," said his mother very calmly.

While she was still binding the leg Frenchie woke
up, spat out the stick and said, hard and clear, "Bring
the cowboys here."

The cowboys were already nearby. Walter Charlie looked at them with no expression whatever on his face. Anatole Harry did not seem to be paying attention one way or the other. Step-and-a-Half Jones, who looked very white beside the two Indians with his shock of silvery hair and his pale, pale blue eyes, was pushing Copenhagen snus into his lower lip. Step-and-a-Half got his nickname by his walk — a thing one seldom saw because he seemed to spend almost all his time on a horse. Many years ago, it was said, Step had broken a leg riding at the far edge of the sprawling Gang Ranch. His horse had left him and he had crawled, dragging the broken leg, for two days before Gang Ranch cowboys happened to find him. The leg never set properly and remained partly bent, so that ever since Step walked a long step with one leg and a half step with the other. Almost everyone considered Step the best cowboy in all the country, and Delore could not understand why his father did not want Step to boss the drive.

Still on saddle horses, all three cowboys moved up beside Frenchie.

Frenchie said, "Delore will boss the drive."

None of the cowboys spoke.

Frenchie said, "Hafter you get that drive to Williams Lake, I will come in and pay you."

"That's okay," said Step. The two Indian cowboys did not speak.

"Now start them," said Frenchie, his voice very faint. "Start them. You're late halready. Delore will come up soon."

The three moved off and in a moment the Bernards could hear them begin to stir the big herd, pushing it toward the saddle of the mountains at the eastern side of the Namko range land, each of the three making their own distinctive sounds. Walter Charlie said, "Chaaaah, chah, chaaah." Step-and-a-Half said, "Hiyu, hi yu, hiiiiy." Anatole Harry talked through his missing teeth.

"Why not Step?" said Delore's mother. "He knows the trail even better than you do, Frenchie."

"Not Step," said Frenchie.

"Well, why not? Delore is too young."

She asked a second time, but Frenchie had fainted again. Delore found the stick and pushed it between his father's teeth once more.

He felt numb, from the top of his head to his heels. All these things were happening much too fast: his father's atrocious pain; his mother's strangely calm voice; the two Indian cowboys and Step, not one of whom seemed to have any feeling about what was happening. They had walked in and out of his field of vision almost like wooden puppets, not like human beings. Nothing about the scene was real. Delore suspected that he was dreaming, that all this would pass in a moment and he would awake in the attic of their log-cabin ranch house with the thin morning sun pushing through the narrow window under the gable roof.

"Delore," said Frenchie.

There was no doubt about how real his father's voice sounded.

"Delore," said Frenchie. This time it was fainter. His

mother looked up from her splinting, her face drawn and worried. Delore noticed that his father still had not drunk any of the whisky.

"Delore," said his father. It was now almost a whisper. Delore moved up and put his head close to his father's.

"Watch for poison parsnip comin' over the saddle into the Happy Ann Meadow," said his father.

Delore nodded.

His father continued, "Stetler will want a cow for crossin' his range. It's dat old canner cow, the brockleface. Make sure that his all 'e takes." Delore nodded. Frenchie half raised himself on his elbows. "Make *sure*," he said, then fell back again. "You understand? He gets that brockleface cow. No other cow. The brockleface."

"What else?" said Delore.

Frenchie screwed up his face. He seemed to be trying to remember something but he was barely afloat at the edge of consciousness. He was silent.

"The pain is very bad," said Delore's mother softly. "Go, Delore."

But Frenchie's eyes opened again. "Use Step," he said. He breathed harshly and seemed for a moment to drop off again. Then he continued in a whisper, "Use Step. *But not too much.*"

"What do you mean?" said Delore.

But his father was silent again.

"You should go, Delore," said his mother.

"What will you do with him?"

"I can load him into the hay wagon. We'll get him

down to the store and a truck will take him in to the hospital."

Delore considered. The store, where the government road ended, was fourteen miles away over the meadows. His mother would have to drive the wagon all that distance, with his father groaning and fainting in the hay behind her. "Can you lift him into the wagon?" he said.

His mother said impatiently, "Of course I can lift him. Take the drive out, Delore."

His mother was a tiny little woman. Even at fifteen, Delore was taller than she was and weighed more. But at this moment she seemed as big and impressive as Frenchie.

"Okay," he said.

He started to walk around the buckskin, which had stood quietly through the whole episode, her reins on the ground, as a good saddle horse should. Half-way to the horse he paused and turned. His father lay with his waxy grey face to the sky. His mother was bent over the broken leg, wrapping it. Delore thought for a moment she might be crying. He walked back to his father, not looking at his mother.

"Dad," he said. He could scarcely remember when he had last called his father "Dad."

Frenchie opened his eyes and looked at a cloud overhead.

"Isn't there anything I can do for you?" said Delore.

His father looked at the cloud for a long time. Then he said, "Yes. Get the hell out of here and leave me alone. I got pain." Delore turned around and walked back to the buckskin mare. Behind him, he heard his father curse again, looking apparently at the split twenty-five-dollar riding boot. "Damn, spoil a good boot."

It was two hundred miles to the stockyards at the Lake, they said, and Delore, numbed and cold as he felt, realized that he might never make it.

WHICH TRAIL?

The drive was already moving east toward the dip in the green timber hill between Namko and Happy Ann Meadow at the top of the Chilcotin River rivershed. Its bawling shook the still morning air and echoed from the wall of lodgepole pines on the edges of the Long Opening. The great, round, brown-and-white swirl of cattle which had been kept in the meadow's centre was now stretching out in a turbulent, noisy stream, pointed toward the east.

As he trotted up on Stella Delore noticed Walter Charlie was riding at the point of the drive. The lead would be a comfortable position on the drive later, when it had shaken down. It would be necessary to make sure that they took it turn about.

Old Step-and-a-Half Jones, half-way down the drive on the lower right side, rode a bay which had two white socks and a blaze on the face. It was, like Step, experienced. It held its head low, kept its eyes on the cattle and spotted those which began to break away from the main herd just as quickly as Step did.

On the drag end, with the dust already blowing about him, was Anatole leading the pack train, which was snorty, and doing his best to prevent homesick cattle from turning back. There were five horses in Anatole's pack train. In the rawhide boxes lashed to their packsaddles they carried most of the grub and all of the canvas, hobbles, rope and assorted gear that the drive would need during the next few weeks. They would also serve as spare saddle horses, although none rated a better name than cayuse. A couple of them had escaped pack work, indeed any sort of work, for a full two years. They had lived on the high meadows, free, almost as the old mustang stock out of Mexico. More than a trace of the mustang still showed in them.

We should have brought more horses, thought Delore as he rode up to join Anatole and ride the drag.

Just before they left the Long Opening he looked back across the buckbrush and the lake of yellow grass which it enclosed. At the far end, nearest the home ranch, he could see the tiny figures of his mother and the horses and his young brother Robbie, who was now bringing up the wagon, but he could no longer make out the figure of his father lying in the grass. Delore had never felt so lonely in his life.

Delore noticed that Anatole sat very flat in the stock saddle—the way he had noticed visitors from Vancouver ride, throwing their weight back on the horse's loin and putting very little weight in the stirrups. Anatole was going to tire that horse quickly and perhaps rub a saddle sore into its back as well. He wanted to tell Anatole to stand in his stirrups, to ride straight up, but decided not to.

Anatole did not have much experience in cowboying. He had spent almost all his life in the Blackwater River country. His people made the best living they could by trapping beaver and shooting squirrels. No road reached them, there were no schools, no doctors—only forest, laced by thin, swampy meadows. Many of the people could speak no English at all. Probably Anatole knew no English until he came out to the Namko country five years ago and began to work as a cowboy for various ranchers.

"Might be we take the low trail, it's best," said Anatole.

"You mean the one by old Sitkum Casmeer's?"

"I think it's good we go that way."

"I dunno. Why?"

"It's good, that trail."

Sometimes, after passing the saddle of the ridge above Happy Ann Meadow, the drive went by a southern trail and stopped overnight at a meadow owned by an old man called Sitkum Casmeer. Sometimes, instead, they kept to a higher trail. In the last two drives Frenchie had kept to the upper trail but he had not said why. Delore wished Frenchie had told him why before he left the Long Opening, but probably his father had been in too much pain to remember.

His father had said, however, to depend on Step-and-a-Half. He'd do that. "But not too much," he also remembered his father saying.

"What way you think?" said Anatole.

"I don't know." They rode on for a minute and Delore added, "I'll make up my mind later. It's two weeks before we get there."

"Sure good, that lower trail," said Anatole.

Delore wished his father were there and that he was just a cowboy on this drive, even if he had only the tiresome chore of leading packhorses most of the day. It would be better than this.

Everything he liked about the Namko drive, the leaves like golden coins held in the thin arms of the poplar groves, the whir of a covey of sharptail grouse where Walter had flushed them out of the buckbrush into the dark green jack pine, even the coyote with the great bush of a tail who spooked to the right through the buckbrush, none of these things seemed familiar and pleasant as they had a mere half hour before. Everything had changed, even Anatole Harry who now looked at him sideways, without moving his head or his eyes, and said, " 'S long way we got to push them cows, ent it, boss?"

Delore did not feel like a boss at all. As if to confirm his feelings, the buckskin mare stumbled. Delore bent in the saddle, throwing his weight in the opposite direction so that she could recover. She recovered. She had stepped into a ground squirrel's hole. She should have noticed the hole. He knew that. So did she. Anybody, man or horse, could see the mound of new yellow earth. But for some reason the little mare had put her right front foot into the hole. Delore remembered what Step-and-a-Half had told him at one time. "If your saddle horse can't tell where to go, get another one," Step had said.

When he looked up he saw that Step was not far away, having let much of the drive pass him. It would be just as well, thought Delore, if Step hadn't noticed Stella tangling her feet. Apparently he had not. Step's face was turned away from him.

But when Delore rode past to join Walter ahead,

Step remarked mildly, "There seems to be a small touch of tanglefoot in that mare, kid."

"I walked her into a hole," said Delore shortly.

Step turned his pale blue eyes toward him and appeared to be digesting a large, new and untested idea. "Oh," said Step.

Delore put Stella into a trot to catch up with Walter Charlie. Behind him, he thought he heard Step's horse also break into a trot, but he did not turn to see.

When he came up beside Walter on the trail ahead Walter said, "Sure long way."

"It's a long way from the home meadow to the Royal Bank," said Delore.

Walter gave a half-smile. "I guess that's good way to say it," he said. He trotted back and to the right to prevent another segment of the herd from breaking into the timber which had now crowded in upon them.

When he came back Delore said, keeping his voice low and casual, "You ride point for the first day, Walter."

"Sure," said Walter in his usual velvety voice.

Delore looked sideways at Walter, who was again half smiling. Walter, he knew, was not a Chilcotin like the other Indians. He could not even talk their language. Ol Antoine, the oldest Indian in Namko, had once said he was a Kispiox and had also said, "Never trust a Kispiox." Why should he remember this now? And what did it amount to, anyway? Probably it was just one of those silly expressions that people picked up. Walter, perhaps, heard it as, "Never trust a Chilcotin." And maybe all the Indians said among themselves, "Never trust a white." But in spite of such reasoning, the words kept running through his head as they walked their horses together toward the far saddle of the hills.

An old cow was leading the drive. That was fortunate; a leader had emerged from the one hundred and ninety-seven head of stock, and before long they could hope all the drive would follow her automatically and the riders could concentrate merely on watching for young or foolish or wilful or just plain stupid animals that wanted to go the wrong way.

When Walter looked toward him Delore kept his face stiff, just like the ears on the buckskin mare.

"I think it's good idea we take that low trail," said Walter.

Now, why did Walter also say this? This was pressure, gentle and strong pressure. The Indian cowboys wanted to take the lower trail. But why?

When Step came up on his horse and asked where they would camp that night, Delore lifted the subject of which trail to take gently into the dusty air. It might be instructive to display the idea before Step when one of the Indian cowboys was present.

"We were wondering whether to take the high trail or the low one," said Delore.

Step looked quickly at Walter. The sun was high and hot and seemed to bleach all the meadow, as it bleached the deadfall sticks bone white. Step's big black hat threw deep shadow over his face, but his unnaturally pale blue eyes seemed to catch the light.

"Don't take that trail past Sitkum Casmeer's, kid," he said.

Delore began to say, "Don't call me kid." Instead he

said, "I'll decide which way we go." Walter looked at him with a sardonic twist of his lips.

"Not by Sitkum's!" said Step.

Walter said, "What does the boss say? That's what counts, I think."

"You just want a shot of that booze he makes," said Step.

"How many times you see me drunk?" asked Walter in a very gentle voice.

Delore could not remember ever seeing Walter drunk, or hearing of his being drunk. He was thinking about this while Step continued in his angry tones, "The curse of booze is what keeps this country down. Dirty, rotten, stinking booze. I tell you, it's the curse of this country."

Walter smiled and quoted, as he sometimes did for reasons hard to understand, from the Bible: "Strong drink is raging." There was a sneer in his voice and Delore noticed Step's neck going red.

Step said, "Listen, Walter, you ain't telling this kid where he's going to go."

"Neither are you," said Delore. He might as well go ahead now, there was no turning back on his earlier words. Step looked at him. Delore looked ahead. "There's some breaking off toward the timber on your side," he said.

Step moved, instantly it seemed, from a walk to a full gallop, moving to cut the group back into the main herd.

"I'd better get to the other side, Walter," said Delore.

"I guess that's right," said Walter. Before Delore

turned the mare Walter added, "You think might be we take that trail past Sitkum Casmeer's?"

"I'll decide later."

Walter shrugged and Delore trotted away.

On the first day they moved ten miles before stopping for the night. They pushed the drive into a little meadow, a nameless meadow as far as Delore knew. It had a swamp along one side. He hoped the cattle would be afraid to tread over this soft ground during the night. On the other sides was tall lodgepole pine, a heavy enough growth for no grass to grow beneath the trees. That should discourage the cattle from ambling off through the trees, feeding as they went.

"I think one man can night herd here all right," said Delore to Anatole. Anatole did not answer.

Step-and-a-Half and Walter rode up, and all four looked at the herd, where the grunting and bawling was fading away as the animals began to feed.

"Who wants to take first shift night herding?" said Delore.

No one answered. After a moment Delore said, "Anatole, will you watch them until dark? Then, Step, you watch them from dark to ten o'clock. And Walter from ten to four . . . and then me." Delore felt his voice going very thin.

Nobody spoke but everybody moved. Walter walked his horse to the far side of the herd. Anatole led the five packhorses to a grassy knoll which stood a few feet above the level of the flat, half-mile-long meadow. Step moved after them.

Anatole said over his shoulder, "I guess it's okay, we camp this place here?"

"Sure, sure. Good place," said Delore, He wished he had pointed out that place to Anatole first. Things seemed to be happening without his having any control over them. He wished it was last year's drive, when his father arranged all these things with a few grunts and nods, and when he himself had no responsibility except to look after his own horse and do his work and not talk too much.

He pulled the saddle off Stella. Beneath, her saddle blanket was damp but not too damp. As he took it away from her he put his hand at her withers. Not too hot.

What would he do, he wondered, if she developed a saddle sore? Ride all the way to Williams Lake turnabout on packhorses? They were poor sorts. But he could not ride Stella if she became saddle-sore — not that, and ever after see her with the white patches near the withers that advertised to everyone who saw her that she had been badly packed or badly ridden.

What if one of the cowboys' horses began to get sore? Anatole sat his horse so badly.... Should he say something? What could he say to another man about another man's horse? What did his father do in such circumstances? He could not remember that the occasion ever arose.

Step and Anatole pulled the diamond hitches off the packs on the other horses. Step threw Delore a set of hobbles, wordlessly. He buckled them about his mare's ankles, stripped off the bridle, hung it on a broken branch of the tree above his saddle and let her

go. Stella, her front feet held just a foot apart by the
hobbles, moved off awkwardly, throwing both front
legs in the air together as she thrust herself forward
with her back legs. It was a long time since Stella had
been hobbled. She would not move fast. Not for the
first few nights. After that, perhaps, she would learn to
move at the pace of a fast-walking man. If she decided
some night to start moving back to Namko, how long
might they have to trail her?

An uneasy wind moved the grass in the meadow. A
grey, ominous sunset was building. Anatole paused a
moment as the wind moved and looked toward the
grey and dirty yellow sky that lay on the broken crust
of the Coast Range.

"Might be it snows," he said.

Wouldn't that be something? Snow in September.
It had happened before. Delore remembered when he
was very young he went with Frenchie into the high
mountain country in July and was caught in a raging
blizzard for four days. The more he thought, the more
his troubles seemed to increase. He said to himself,
"When you don't know what to do, do some work."

"You talking to me?" said Step.

"No," said Delore.

He picked a hand axe from the jumble of gear pulled
down from the packhorses. He split a few pieces from
a jagged stump nearby, where wind or snow had
snapped off one of the pines. Carefully he split a dozen
pieces of the yellow, resinous wood, pieces about a
foot long, a quarter of an inch thick, two or three inches
wide. He pulled his hunting knife from the sheath
at his belt and began to shave feathers, four to five

inches long, at the sides of each sliver. When he had done six of them he pulled the waterproof match case from the front pocket of his jeans. He lit one, holding the feathers downward, and watched the yellow fire move gracefully up the wood. Laying this on the ground, he touched another feather stick to the flame, let it catch, laid it atop the other. One by one, he laid the feather sticks in a pile, then added heavier pieces of wood. Soon the fire crackled. When a fire began to snap, a camp was begun, never before the fire snapped, but as soon as it snapped.

Step was laying the canvas tarp lean-to style, like one side of a sloping roof, one edge at the ground pegged by short ropes, the upper edge held about four feet high by ropes to nearby trees. It faced toward the fire. During the night the men sleeping would lie in their bags with their faces toward the dying fire, their feet at the narrow end of the lean-to, and the dirty white canvas would reflect some of the heat toward their faces until the fire died.

Delore decided it was time to tell somebody, Walter perhaps, to get wood for the night's fire. But when he looked up, Walter was already moving away with the big double-bitted axe in his hand. Step watched him go, then looked at Delore. He walked over in his broken-gaited way and squatted on his heels beside the fire, holding out his hands to the flame. A thin white scar ran from Step's left eye to his chin. Delore could not remember noticing this about Step before. Step-and-a-Half had been in the Namko country for so many years he seemed like a part of the scenery.

After a while Step said, "It's a long drive, kid."

"Yeah."

"You're sure young for bossing a beef drive." There did not seem to be anything to say, so Delore did not say it. After a while Step continued, "Was a time years ago, I cowboyed for the greatest cowman of them all. Old Danger, we used to call him. I remember him telling me once what made a good cow boss." Step looked at his rough hands. "He says to me, 'A good boss always sees everything he is sposed to see. And he don't ever see anything he ain't sposed to see.'"

There did not seem anything to say to this either.

Step touched Delore's shoulder with his hand. "It's okay, kid, we'll get them all in there. And without running a pound of fat off them neither." He stood up. Delore sensed there was something more that Step wanted to tell him. There was.

"I guess we'll take the upper trail, eh, kid."

"I don't know. There's a lot of slide rock on that high trail. We might have some go lame."

"Upper trail's best. Way better."

Walter Charlie, who had returned dragging some bleached white deadfall logs behind him, paused to listen.

"If it snows," said Delore, "it'll be worse on the high trail."

"I think might be it snows," said Walter.

"Who asked you?" said Step sharply, and then again to Delore, "Upper trail's the only way, only safe way."

Walter, with a half smile on his face, said, "Oh, that lower trail's pretty good, I think."

"The upper trail," said Step harshly.

Delore said, "I don't have to decide for a long time yet."

He got on his feet, conscious of both men watching him. He walked toward the heaped up pack boxes. They were cased in iron-hard dried cowhide from which most of the brown and white hair had, many years ago, worn away to the yellow untanned skin. "I guess we better get some supper started."

"I get some more wood," said Walter.

Anatole came forward at his slow pace and began to pull bacon, beans and coffee from the pack boxes.

Step said, under his breath, "I am talking to you in the head, kid. Take the high trail. Don't go the bottom way."

STAMPEDE

Because the clock inside his head was working in its usual mysterious way, Delore was awake in his sleeping bag at 3.45 A.M. but he lay there, pretending to be asleep, until Walter Charlie came to shake him about a quarter past four. Then he spoiled it all by being stiff, and Walter gave just one twitch to his shoulder before saying, flat voiced, "You're awake. It's okay."

"Yeah. Okay."

Delore pulled himself out of the bag. He wore only his shorts. Always he had been told that to sleep in any more of your clothes was a mistake, because the steam from your body was trapped in the clothing overnight and you started the day damp. Apparently Step did not care about such rules. He looked at the old cowboy from the light of a blazing fresh stick that Walter had tossed on the dull fire. Step had never acquired a down-filled sleeping bag but used what was called a blanket roll, a long quilted wool blanket. When Step went to bed he started at one lower corner of the blanket roll and rolled his body over until he had as many folds about himself as he judged the night's temperature required. Delore noticed that Step's feet, still in the well-worn, scuffed riding boots, stuck out from the end of the blanket roll.

Only a little patch of coal-black, coarse hair showed above the top of Anatole Harry's bag, which was a poor, thin, silk-covered thing bought from a mail-order house in Vancouver. "All shine and no warmth," Step had remarked when Anatole got into it that night.

"Almost all them cattle's lying down," said Walter. He sat on his sleeping bag. He pulled off his pants, his boots and his shirt. Walter had the finest sleeping bag of any of them. It was a Royal Canadian Air Force survival-kit bag, all pure eiderdown, according to the tag, thick as a mattress and soft as a pile of hay. It was still stamped with the broad arrow and the encircling C, which meant that it was Canadian government property. Delore wondered how Walter got the bag. He was going to ask but he remembered what Step had told him about a good boss never seeing what he was not supposed to see, so he said nothing.

It was cold. There was a small wind.

He was shivering as he got into his denim jacket, his pants, his stiff, cold boots. All, like the grass, were clammy. The thin flame had begun to die on the stick that Walter had tossed into the campfire. Walter slipped quickly into his sleeping bag, pulled his rolled pants under his head for a pillow and, in an instant it seemed, was sleeping. Delore walked the mare around the herd for what seemed to be not hours but days. Most were standing but a few, here and there, were lying on the cold grass. That, at least, was a good sign, that cattle would lie down.

He remembered Frenchie telling him once, in one of his father's typically short and unembroidered conversations, that he had once spent a year in Durango in

Mexico. Frenchie did not say why he went to Mexico or why he left, but that was Frenchie's way. The one thing his father seemed to remember was that the cattle and the donkeys never lay down.

"All their lives they keep walking and eating," Frenchie had said. "They never have time to lie down. There ain't enough feed. All the time they are on their feet eating."

Remembering this, Delore felt better as he and the mare walked around the edges of the beef drive. His stock were not restless. His stock were at rest. He thought of the day, three weeks from today, perhaps, when they would be pushing them down the gravel road that led into Williams Lake from the old, creaking Sheep Creek suspension bridge on the muddy Fraser River. Tourist cars would be pulled in at the side of the road as the drive went through. Perhaps someone from Vancouver or the States would say, "Pardon me, what is this?" and he would answer, very casually, "This is the Namko drive, Ma'am." And then he would ride on without telling them that the drive had come two hundred miles, more or less, across the big plateau and that almost all of it had been travelled away from the roads.

Once, he remembered, one of the Vancouver newspapers had sent a reporter and a photographer to meet his father when the drive came into Williams Lake, but Frenchie had ignored them, as he ignored bankers and other people whom he did not understand. Frenchie had just answered "Yes" and "No" to their questions, and after a while the two newspapermen shrugged their shoulders and gave up trying to get information from Frenchie. They took a few pictures of the drive funnelling into the Holding Ground above the town, and one of the pictures later appeared in the paper with the words, "Long Beef Drive Ends." The caption had continued: " 'Frenchie' Bernard, boss of the Namko beef drive, longest on the North American continent, reported 'nothing unusual' when he brought 215 head into Williams Lake Sunday." Although he could not remember his father using these words, Delore decided he would say the same: " 'Nothing unusual,' said Delore Bernard Sunday, etc. etc."

Reluctantly, it seemed, light filled the sky. There was heavy cloud cover but not heavy enough to drop rain or snow on the meadow. If it were not going to snow, perhaps they should take the upper trail. Delore crossed his arms across the horn of the saddle. His head fell forward a little. He dozed. His head fell forward until the cords at the back of his neck twitched. When he threw back his head, his hat almost fell off. He grabbed at it clumsily, half asleep, and knocked it off his head to the grass. Delore stepped off Stella, forgetting he was near several steers, which were lying half hidden in the tall grass.

The steers had not had a man come close to them afoot since the bloody day on which they had been branded with the sizzling hot irons, and had a wattle knifed in their cheeks as a further identifying mark, and been castrated. This they remembered, however vaguely. Pain and confusion and fright were associated with a man on foot. They remembered nothing so painful in association with the double figure on four legs. (Did they know it for a man and a horse or did they consider it a third type of animal, neither man nor horse? Who could say?)

Bawling, they got to their feet, hind ends first, awkwardly, then up from their front knees, then, with the speed of deer it seemed, charging into the main herd. By the time Delore was back on Stella all the drive seemed to have broken loose. Some were stampeding back over the trail that they had taken the previous day. Those were the first to stop. He ran Stella standing in the stirrups, to turn them before they reached the camp. They turned. In the eye of the fading campfire he saw Step unroll from his bedroll and come out boots and all, and start automatically toward his big bay horse which grazed nearby.

Step paused just long enough to land a solid kick on both the other cowboys in their bags and say, "Stampede!"

An old cow ran toward him, her tail straight out behind her with one kink in it. Seeing Step she paused, glared wildly about her and whirled, to thunder off in the opposite direction.

Delore swept into the timber, holding his face down so that dead branches could not switch into his eye. There were many one-eyed cowboys in this country. Riding into timber was always dangerous. He distinguished three vague forms from under the brim of his cowboy hat, yipped at them and turned them back on the grass. When he rode out on the meadow a minute later he saw that both Walter and Anatole were catching their horses. Step had a halter on his bay and, riding bareback, galloped toward the far end of the meadow.

Anatole pulled himself aboard his horse, using the

mane. He was thrown off. He got on again and this time held his seat, trotted her to the camp and got off to put on the bridle and saddle which he had left on a fallen tree the night before.

"What in God's green world is stupider than a cow?" shouted Step, as he went past Delore at a fast trot. It made Delore feel better.

It also made him feel better when he noticed that most of the drive were not racing for the timber but milling, confused and noisy, at the centre of the meadow. They would stay there. It would be only the wilder stock, just brought in during the past few days from the alpine meadows of the highest summer range, that would be so foolish, so crazy in the head, that they would try to leave the main herd. An hour later the four riders had all the drive back in the meadow. Delore's cheek was bleeding from a stick which he had brushed in one of his races through the jack pines. Step's shirt was torn and his horse was wet with sweat.

Delore was counting. It was now full light. He counted several times and got the numbers 192, 204 and 196. It was hard to count so many animals.

"They're all there," said Step. He pulled out his round pillbox of snus and tucked some in his lower lip.

Delore started counting again.

"I don't think this cowboying life is for me," said Step. He spat beside his horse's left foot, considered some more and said, "Me, I think I am going to learn to read and write. Then I'll be a lawyer."

"What is that bunch doing at the far end of the meadow?" said Delore.

They looked. A ring of cows had formed near the swamp, watching something.

"Look like they're watching a coyote," said Step. "They ring around coyotes with their heads forward."

"Anatole's beyond them there."

"Yeah. I guess he is, too. We better go down see."

They rode down the meadow. Walter remained at the far edge of the drive, walking his horse, watching the cattle. When Step and Delore reached the ring of curious animals at the far end, they found the old brockleface which was to be paid to Stetler. She had let confusion and fright lead her into the swamp. Her legs were out of sight, her belly was deep in the mud. The whites of her eyes showed, she slavered at the mouth.

Anatole had a rope about her horns. Not only was the brockleface one of the oldest and thinnest cows of the drive, she had also in some way escaped being dehorned at her branding time, some many years ago. Probably she was one of the first cows which they tried to dehorn by placing tight rubber bands at the base of the horns, so that the horns of young heifers withered and finally fell off. Most ranchers used the rubber band method to take the horns off their stock, but it had required some time of experimentation before this method became a success. The brockleface had grown her horns despite the band. The horns were poor and ugly, as was she herself.

Anatole had roped her about the horns, dallied the other end to the horn of his saddle and was now trying to drag her free of the mud. The cow was stuck too deeply. Soon, if they did not free the terrified beast, she would become so weary that her head would drop into the mud through the thin green grass, and she would drown there.

"One more horse will bring her out," said Step.

Delore rode close to the boghole, felt Stella shiver in fear beneath him, flipped his noose from the saddle and saw it settle about the crooked horns on the first throw.

"Not bad," said Step. Step was still riding bareback. He had no saddle, no rope.

Anatole had kept the tension on his rope. Delore now walked Stella forward, taking a dally about the saddle horn as she moved. Both ropes tightened and the two horses began to crouch on their legs so that they might pull heavily.

"One thing . . ." said Step.

Anatole and Delore paused to look at him. Step wiped some dark brown spittle from the right corner of his mouth. They waited.

"Which one's she gonna charge?" said Step.

Delore was not sure what Step meant. He could not tell if Anatole knew or not; probably not, because Anatole knew little about horses and cows, being a "stick Indian" from the Blackwater. Step spat again. "That old cow ain't just scared," he said, "she's mad, too, because she's in there. Once she gets out she is gonna look for somebody to blame for her being in there. I guess it is going to be one of you two."

"We'll move opposite ways, once she starts to come out," said Delore. He looked across at Anatole. Anatole nodded.

Both dug their heels into their horses. The ropes

strained. The brockleface cow snorted, heaved, humped her back, strained and, with the mud gulping at her legs, came free. Delore rode right. Anatole forgot. Instead, he stopped his horse. The cow charged him. Delore tried to move quickly in the opposite direction to take up tension on his rope, but there was no time. Anatole's horse jumped to avoid the snorting old cow and Anatole went out of the saddle.

She butted Anatole once with her crooked horns. He fell backward and she started again toward him. Delore was still backing his horse away to tighten the rope and stop her charge. Then he realized that he had loosed his hold on the rope end and the dally had lifted free of his saddle horn. He had no control of the cow whatever. Almost as the realization came to him, Step flashed between him and Anatole.

Step slipped off his bareback horse, grabbed the two twisted horns of the brockleface and began to twist her head. He could not control her. His heels dug furrows in the sod as she dragged him, but there was time for Anatole to roll away from beneath her charge and join Step in grabbing her head. Before Delore could dismount and run to help them, they had twisted her neck so that it seemed it would break. It did not break, she relaxed and let them roll her to her back. They pulled the ropes free from her and stepped quickly away to their horses and remounted.

The old cow rolled back to her feet and stood. She seemed to have forgotten all her rage, all her panic. Delore stepped back into the saddle. They watched her a moment. She puffed, blew sputum from her nostrils, and then ambled toward the main herd.

"I guess she don't like us so good," said Anatole.

"Like I say," said Step, "I figure I have got to learn to be a lawyer. This cowboy business is too strenuous for me."

They walked their horses back to camp. The old cow in the boghole was not mentioned again, but Delore wished he had kept his line tight on the saddle horn, particularly when two of his men were there to notice. Worst of all, neither Step nor Anatole mentioned that the boss had loosed his rope too soon.

"HIDE YOUR BRIDLES"

During the next four days nobody mentioned the old brockleface being stuck in the boghole or anything else about that incident, although Step said more than once that he suspected there must be better ways to earn a living than by cowboying. The drive had shaken down well. The first old cow to take the lead had fallen back and been replaced by an older, leaner cow that appeared to be half Hereford, half Angus. The new leader walked the trail as if she had been over it before. This could not be so, yet she seemed to know when to leave the track and cut through poplar or pine groves to avoid deadfalls across the trail. Once, at the edge of what appeared to be a fine meadow, she balked completely when Anatole tried to make her lead the drive across it. Anatole found why when he rode his own horse out a few yards and it sank to the hocks, so that he had to dismount and coax it back from the muskeg.

Anatole's saddle horse had started a saddle sore, as Delore had feared, but Anatole had switched to one of the stockier packhorses, which seemed to bear up well under him. Anatole's saddle horse had joined the pack train, empty. The four other horses carried extra loads without complaint.

There was little talk.

Sometimes Anatole or Walter remarked again about the advantages of taking the lower trail past Sitkum Casmeer's, and frequently Step-and-a-Half commented on the evils of alcohol and told how, as a fourteen-year-old boy, he took the pledge never to drink, at a religious meeting held under a tent at Penticton in the Okanagan Valley.

"There I gave myself to my Saviour," said Step, one night at the campfire. Although Step did not talk much—sometimes, it seemed, he did not say ten words in a whole day—when he did talk his voice was strong and stirring, like the sound of an organ.

"Funny thing," Walter had said. "You give up your soul, but ain't nobody takes it." He paused, seemed to consider this curious situation for a moment and then said, "Not even when it's free."

"You are an unbeliever," said Step. "You are the anti-Christ."

"Time for supper!" Delore had shouted, very loudly, and as Anatole served up the usual beans and bacon the other two men had taken their tin plates and squatted beside the night fire—Step white, his lips quivering, Walter with the usual half-smile showing beneath opaque blue-black eyes that never seemed to show any smile at all.

Daily now, each man undertook his own share of the work without explicit orders being given. Anatole was packer and cook and occasionally helped herd also, as well as he could while leading the pack train. Step-

and-a-Half Jones, Walter and Delore alternated positions on the drive, one man in the comfortable position at the point, a second moving back and forth along the sides of the drive, and a third in the most disliked position of all—at the back, "riding the drag" in the dust from one hundred and ninety-seven sets of hooves. Each night Step stretched the tarp for their lean-to, Walter cut wood, Delore circled the drive until supper time, and through the nights they kept the same watches as they had established the first night out of Namko. Every man seemed a little thinner, even in only four days. Step said this was because Anatole couldn't cook well enough to suit a hungry crab, to which Anatole, who had never seen a crab, would respond with his usual gap-toothed smile. Delore looked forward to putting the drive inside Stetler's fencing the fifth night out.

That night there would be no night herding. Fences would contain the drive. That was the reason that Stetler each year was given one cow from the beef drive, because all the animals fed for two full days on the grass of Stetler's range. When he first learned of this arrangement, it seemed to Delore that Stetler was given a high price for just two nights' grazing, but looking at the old, thin cow that he was to deliver to Stetler, he estimated that it was probably a fair enough exchange.

He was thinking this when he joined Step at the drag end late in the hot afternoon of the day they entered Stetler's range. The drive had crossed some alkali flats and the dirty grey cloud of dust that they pulled behind them had coated Step's face and hands and clothing to a single monotonous colour. The flour-like dust was a fog through which the red disc of the sun cut only dimly. It filled the nostrils and ground in a man's teeth.

"This little girl," said Step, "she says to her mother, 'Mama, do cowboys eat grass?' Her mother says, 'Don't be silly, dear. Cowboys are part human.'"

Delore smiled and they rode together in the dust cloud behind the herd.

"At least tonight we'll be inside Stetler's fence," he said.

"Hide your bridles," said Step, "here comes Stetler."

"Whatya mean by that, Step?"

"You never hear about Stetler?"

"I know he's about the biggest rancher in the country."

"Your dad knows him. Knows him good."

Delore waited and Step spoke again.

"Y'ever hear of starting a ranch with a long rope and a running iron?"

"That's from the old days, ain't it? They used to rope other people's cattle and change the brands with a running iron . . ."

"I figured you knew."

"But Mr. Stetler ain't a rustler."

Step considered. "No. Not exactly. I don't think he has ever changed any brands. Not so far as I know, that is . . ." Step considered some more. "Stetler had a kind of different way. Way Stetler worked, first he earned a dollar. When he was about four or five years old, I guess. Then he made up his mind he wouldn't ever let go of that dollar. He would just get another dollar to add to it."

"That's just thrift," said Delore.

"Yeah, that's one way of calling it," said Step. "But it ain't much better than rustling. Also," he added, "he does borrow, Stetler. He will borrow and forget to return a thing."

"You mean he steals?"

"I never said such a thing. Steal? Stetler? Certainly not. He is thrifty. That's one mark against him. And he will borrow. But I spose we all got faults," Step continued, gently.

Delore wondered if Step was making jokes.

"Last year we went through," said Step, "I was missing my brand-new lariat when we left Stetler's place."

"Did he take it, you mean?"

"No. He wouldn't do that. But he might of borrowed it."

"Then you can ask him for it when we go through tomorrow."

"I will do no such thing," said Step.

"Well, why?"

Step peered through the dust. "There's some drifting left up there," he said, and kicked his horse to a trot. As he left, the words drifted over his shoulder. "All I say is, here's Stetler, so watch your bridles."

Delore remembered this while he counted the last of the one hundred and ninety-seven cattle through the gate of Stetler's home ranch pasture. Stetler had walked his horse up behind him very quietly, and sat leaning forward on the saddle horn, watching as the

last few animals skittered past. Then Anatole walked
the pack train through and Step got off his horse to
close the gate, dragging the usual deep furrow in the
ground with the gate. All gates in the Cariboo sagged,
even Stetler's.

" 'Lo, Mr. Stetler."

Stetler nodded, to indicate he heard, but did not
answer. Stetler had thin lips, thin hips, thin eyes and
wore a thin shirt and thin pants. Even his horse was
thin.

Delore said, "I guess the weather's going to break,
ain't it?" He looked up at the milky sky. The cloud had
been thinner each day. Soon, it seemed, the blue Cariboo sky would wipe off the last of the cloud. Stetler
looked at the sky but did not answer.

"I'll go over and help make camp," said Step. He
got on his horse and left.

Delore stayed by Stetler in uncomfortable silence.
"It hasn't been too bad so far," he said.

Stetler spoke. His voice was like the creaking of the
gate. Perhaps it was because he lived all alone and had
no one to speak with, but Delore remembered that
Stetler's voice was always harsh. "Where's Frenchie?"
he said.

"He couldn't come." Stetler did not ask why, so
Delore felt he had to add an explanation. "He broke
his leg."

"Drunk?"

"No, no. He was riding that big Morgan he got at
Williams Lake and I guess he pushed him too hard in
the swampy ground . . ."

"That's just like him," said Stetler, using the same coarse, flat voice.

"I got your cow, Mr. Stetler."

Stetler looked over the herd, which was now dispersing on the grass of the home ranch pasture. Delore pointed to the brockleface. "It's that one over there. My dad said that was for you."

Stetler just looked.

"I'll cut her out for you now, if you like. I can take her over to your corral. . . ."

Stetler looked some more. Then he said, "Don't bother." He reined his horse around and kicked her into a trot, saying as he left, "I'll cut her out myself later on."

Delore turned toward the edge of the meadow where their camp would be set. Step, he found, had not ridden there but had sat his horse a few yards distant during the conversation with Stetler.

"He's kind of sour, ain't he?" said Delore.

"I thought he was real talkative for Stetler," said Step. "Maybe he likes you, he talks so much."

Step smiled, so did Delore. It was nice to have someone as calm and sensible as Step around when you were fifty miles from home with one hundred and ninety-seven cows. He wondered when Stetler would cut out the old cow and put her in his corral.

NEW CHAPS AND AN
EXTRA PACKHORSE

Because the drive was now all within fencing and because he knew the fencing was good, having circled to check it the night before, there was no need for Delore to awaken in the cold hour before dawn the next morning. Nevertheless he did.

His eyes seemed to spring open. He started to draw himself out of the warmth of his bag, remembered that there was no night herding this night and settled back with relief, dragging the mouth of the bag about his nose to shut out even the slightest breath of the frosty air. The grass beside his head was white with frost, he noticed. He looked at the frost in the white light of the moon, which shone out of a clear, black-blue sky, and prepared himself to drift slowly back to sleep again. His eyes travelled further, to Walter's big, warm bag. How thin it seemed to lie. It was hard to believe that even a lean body like Walter's lay within it. His eyes opened wider. The bag was flat.

Delore raised himself on one elbow and saw clearly that Walter was not there. Now, why?

Walter had left camp the night before, quietly. He

50

was taking a small ride, he said. Not far. None of the others paid any attention, not even when Walter was still absent half an hour later when they went to sleep. Perhaps he was riding down to Stetler's ranch house on some errand or other. But now it was four in the morning, and Walter had not returned. Delore rolled toward Walter's bag and placed his hand inside it. It was cold.

He sat up, still cased in his bag, and held his hands about his knees. The cattle were scattered about the big meadow. There was no light in Stetler's log-cabin ranch house, which stood a hundred yards from their camp, half hidden in trees. Why was Stetler so unfriendly? He hadn't even asked them to visit him for a cup of tea. At least when Frenchie brought the drive through, he and Stetler usually spent half an hour together, drinking strong black tea and talking beef prices. But last night Stetler had just unsaddled his horse, gone indoors, pumped a few puffs of blue smoke from the pipe in making his own supper and then, even before Delore's crew slept, the yellow light of the kerosene lamp had gone out at Stetler's window.

Walter wouldn't be at Stetler's cabin. It was after Stetler's light went out that Walter had saddled his horse and ridden away with his indifferent explanation. Was Anatole gone, too? He looked and saw Anatole's black hair showing at the upper edge of the mound his body made in the bag. And beyond him, Step . . . But Step's bag also was empty. There was something very strange about this night, even though the moon was full and bright and the drive was safe and at peace.

Delore got out, pulled on his boots and his clothes. Gently stepping around the sleeping Anatole, he pushed his hand inside Step's bedroll. This one was still warm. Step had left it only a short time before. Perhaps he had been wakened, without realizing it, by the noises of Step's departure. The fire was completely cold. No new wood had been poured upon it and no new coffee boiled. At the opposite side of the Stetler cabin he could see the corral into which they had put their horses for the night.

There were horses there. He could not see how many.

Between the corral and the shed was another old log cabin, sod-roofed and sagging. It was the first ranch house built on the Stetler place. When the newer cabin had been built it became a shed where Stetler kept saddles, rigging, welding equipment, ropes, mower parts and all the other paraphernalia that went with ranch work. Did he see something move across the empty window of the old place? Delore walked very quietly toward the shed. The moon cast a hard shadow of him on the whitened grass. At the corner of the cabin he stopped, hearing a stirring within. Edging toward the door, he looked inside. A figure moved across the back of the shed. By the walk he knew him.

"Step?" he whispered.

Step stopped, very still. Then he said, also in a whisper, "What you doing here, kid?"

"What're *you* doing here?"

"That's my business."

Delore stepped inside and the darkness and the musty smell of old leather surrounded them both. "I want to know what you're doing here," he said.

They stood very close. Step said softly, "D'ya remember what I said, kid? Always see everything you got to see and don't see anything you don't have to see."

"I'm responsible," said Delore.

Step gave a small sigh, almost a laugh. "I guess that's right, kid." Step put a hand on Delore's shoulder. Old Step was a friendly man. You could not help but feel better when you were near him.

"I tell ya, kid. All I'm doing is looking for my lariat I left last year. You remember I said about it? Well, I'm looking for it."

"At this time of night?"

"What difference? It's mine, ain't it?"

"Also, where's Walter?"

"Well, I guess he went down to that Indian camp."

"What camp?"

"The one we passed a couple of miles other side of the fence. It was about a quarter mile back from that little chain of lakes."

"I didn't see it."

"You still ain't looking at the right things," said Step. He turned his back and began to rummage in a pile of old leather harness by the side of the shed. Delore watched for a moment, then turned and walked quietly back to his sleeping bag. He did not go to sleep for a long time but when he last saw Step-and-a-Half's bag it was still empty.

The sun was hot on his face when Step stirred him with the toe of his boot next morning. "Let's go, trail boss," said Step. When Delore sat up Step passed him a mug of coffee. Everything, he saw, was packed. The tarp had been taken down from over his head without his noticing it. The pack train was already far up the home meadow, led by Anatole. He saw Walter, slapping his chaps, starting the slow tide of the drive moving again. Stella, the mare, was saddled and waiting for him. Step's horse also waited, fully rigged.

Delore drank the coffee so fast it burned his throat, pulled on his clothes and stepped into the saddle. What made him sleep so long? Why should he wake at four in the morning, yet sleep when the day's work needed to be done?

Step was already moving off, taking one packhorse as he went. Apparently Anatole had taken only four packhorses. He looked for Anatole but trees, he saw, hid him and the pack train. Delore was still rubbing the gritty corners of sleep from his eyes five minutes later when Step and the packhorse and his own mare suddenly stopped. Stetler had moved out from a clump of spruce that stood, a green island on the yellow lake of grass, just beside where the drive was slowly passing. Stetler wore the same clothes and the same expression as yesterday afternoon.

"You gonna take your cow now, Mr. Stetler?" said Delore.

Stetler eyed him coldly. "I already took him." His lips tightened even more and he said, "You're boss on this drive. You don't notice when a cow's gone?"

Step said, "We slept in. We gotta hurry now."

"Hurry then," said Stetler.

Step kicked his horse into a trot. The packhorse

shuffled after him. Delore and the mare began to ride by when Stetler said, "Hey, just a minute."

Delore saw that Stetler's eyes were on a pair of fine, golden-tan, silver-buckled chaps, which were showing beneath the canvas of the pack on the horse Step led. Stetler's eyes were on the pack, Step having stopped the horses despite an apparent inclination to keep riding, but Stetler talked to Delore, not to Step.

"Don't rush," said Stetler.

The three riders and four horses stood.

"I ain't asked how your dad is," said Stetler.

"He broke his leg."

"Oh, yes. That's right. How's your mother?"

"Fine."

"And your brothers?"

"Which ones?"

"How many you got?"

"Three."

"Well, how's the oldest?"

"Fine."

Stetler pinched his thin lower lip and looked again at the chaps on the packhorse.

"Them's nice chaps, there," he said.

Where had those chaps come from?

"Yes," said Delore, "they're nice."

"You don't see many chaps like that in this country," said Stetler.

"No, I guess not."

"Used to have a pair like that myself," said Stetler. He waited, but Delore did not answer. Stetler was looking meaner by the moment, but his voice became softer as his eyes became harder. "But I lost them."

"That's too bad," said Delore.

"But them are *your* chaps," said Stetler.

Before Delore could answer, Step did, in just the easy, soft tone of voice that Stetler had used.

"Them's my chaps," said Step.

"Oh. Yours."

"That's right. Mine."

Stetler looked at Delore, then at Step.

"I wonder," he said, very mildly, "I wonder if you would mind telling me just where you got them chaps?"

"No," said Step. "No, I wouldn't mind telling you ..." He waited before continuing. So did Stetler, and so did Delore, who felt more uncomfortable with each passing second. "I tell you how I got them chaps," said Step. He leaned forward on his horse and looked very directly into Stetler's eyes. "I traded, with a guy I know, for one lariat."

Stetler pinched his lower lip very hard, so hard that when he pulled his fingers away a white patch showed and faded only slowly. He appeared about to speak again, but again he pinched his lip. Then he lifted his thin shoulders in a shrug, looked at the ears of Delore's horse and said, apparently to the mare, "Well . . . it would be my opinion that you got the best of the deal." Looking to Delore, he raised one hand. "Luck," he said, and rode back toward his ranch house.

For the next fifteen minutes Delore could see laughter bubbling up under Step's shoulder blades, but the old cowboy never let a sound escape his lips.

They were in thick timber very soon, and all busy keeping the drive confined to the narrow rocky trail.

An hour later Delore discovered that Stetler had taken a good steer, and left the thin useless old brockleface cow to walk out to Williams Lake with the drive, if she could.

Also, he discovered that somehow the drive had acquired an extra packhorse, complete with saddle and load. Anatole was leading one too many horses.

THE OUTLAW HORSE

Delore trotted forward to look at the extra packhorse. It was second of the string, an Appaloosa, one of the best Delore had ever seen.

The Appaloosas were first brought to North America by the Spaniards, according to the encyclopaedia he had read at home, but they were developed by a tribe of very turbulent Indians in the Oregon Territory of the United States—the Nez Perces. Good in the withers, lean, they were solid coloured at the front usually, and spotted white on the rump.

"The ideal horse for an outlaw," his father had told him once. "When you go into the trees, the rump blends in with the light coming through those leaves."

Delore remembered this as he walked beside the tough stringy Appaloosa. It was disturbing to think of the new packhorse as an outlaw's horse, even if the wars of the Nez Perces and the American cavalry were long gone and long forgotten by most people.

"Whose horse?" he asked Anatole.

"I think, might be, it's Walter's," said Anatole. Nothing was very positive with Indians and they began or ended almost every sentence with the words, "Might be," or "I think," or "Spose maybe."

"What's he want with another packhorse?"

"I guess I don't know that thing," said Anatole.

Delore slowed his horse until the Appaloosa came abreast of him again. He looked at the pack boxes. They were old, old boxes. One hung each side of the packsaddle. Each was about two feet long, two feet high and a foot wide. They were wrapped in untanned cowhide which was as hard as metal, dirty yellow rawhide crosscrossed by wrinkles and scratches. He could almost, but not quite, distinguish a brand on one hide. How old were these, he wondered. It would not surprise him if they were fifty, or even seventy-five years old. He noticed one other thing. The lids were tied down like a Christmas package. Clearly Walter did not intend to let anyone know what was inside.

A horse ahead whinnied. Delore looked ahead. Walter had been waiting for the train to come past, standing his own horse in the shade of some poplar. By remaining completely motionless upon his motionless horse Walter had remained undetected by Delore or Anatole. It was Anatole's horse which had first seen or smelt the other horse in the rustling poplars.

"I don't see you," said Anatole, but he said nothing more and the pack train walked past. Walter fell in with it on the opposite side of the Appaloosa from Delore and, three abreast, they moved on at a slow walk.

"What do we need with another packhorse, Walter?"

Walter thought before answering. "I take that packhorse for a friend I got," he said.

"To where?"

Walter thought some more. "Might be he's camped on this trail."

"Might be? What if he isn't?"

"I don't know."

"What friend? Who is he?"

"He's man I meet loooooong time ago," said Walter. Then he said nothing more. Sometimes, when older Indians told stories and used the long-drawn-out "loooooong" they would pause for a minute or more to indicate that it was, indeed, a very long time ago. But Walter was not doing this, apparently. Delore realized Walter did not intend to tell him who the friend was. Well, did it matter? Frenchie used to say, "Before you ask a question of hanother man, ask yourself a question first: 'Is it any of my business?' "

Delore asked himself this question now, decided it wasn't, and said, "Well, I guess it's a good thing to have an extra horse in the string."

"Better I go up see how them cows is moving," said Walter. He touched his heels to his horse and was quickly gone.

Delore rode beside the Appaloosa for a few more minutes. It had been branded, he saw, at the shoulder, and not with a branding iron. The brand had been clumsily traced with the end of a running iron, such as rustlers used in the old days and some Indians still used today. With a running iron one could trace any brand one wished, but usually it made a wavy, irregular mark and, because the tip of the iron cooled too quickly, the brand varied in intensity where the cooling iron failed to burn much deeper than the horse's hair. Part of this brand faded to nothingness and he could not read it. It was, perhaps, an M, but was that a straight line traced above it—in which case it would be a Bar M brand—or was it a curved line, which would read as the Rocking M? And, anyway, what ranch had Bar M or Rocking M brands? For the past several years all brands had been required to carry three, instead of two, distinguishing features.

Clearly this horse was not from the Namko country. But the M reminded him of something, something that his mind could not quite seize. Who was branding with an M at the centre some twelve or fifteen years ago? For that matter, was it an M?

The black mare who led the pack train pulled back her ears and kicked at Stella. She was a bad-tempered old animal, and always had been. Stella skipped out of the way, so that the hoof barely touched her flank. Delore trotted her ahead to the drive. That was his business. Strange packhorses were not.

THE CALMNESS OF
STEP-AND-A-HALF JONES

Before they had been many days on the Beef Trail
Delore realized that Anatole was slow to understand
things and, in fact, not to put too fine a word on it,
stupid. Of course he could not read or write, but that
was not Anatole's fault. He had never had the oppor-
tunity to learn. He had undoubtedly begun shooting
squirrels to help make money for his hungry family's
funds as early as eight years of age, and to this day, so
far as Delore knew, Anatole had never seen a neon
sign or a paved sidewalk or a refrigerator or a room
with a carpet on the floor. All these things were unknown to Anatole because he had never been as far
from home as Williams Lake. However, Delore himself
had never been farther from home than the Lake, so he
himself knew about trolley buses, jet airliners and big
department stores only by reading about them. Anatole, however, seemed unable to understand even
ordinary things at times.

The only salad stuffs, so-called, carried on the pack
train were canned tomatoes, which Frenchie had
bought at the Namko general store. These, with bacon
and beans and rice, were the staple diet for the beef

drive crew. Sometimes they liked the tomatoes cold. Then they opened a can and slopped the thing over their tin plates. But occasionally, when the night winds were chill, Step and Walter would ask for hot tomatoes. Anatole's action never varied. He stood a can of tomatoes in the hot coals at the edge of the campfire to heat, but he could not remember to cut a small hole in the tin first. As the paper crisped away from the sides and the picture of the bright red tomatoes withered to black ash, steam would build inside the can. Finally it would explode.

On the third occasion Step suggested mildly, as Anatole placed the can in the coals, "I really do think it would be better to open that tin some first." But Anatole did not seem to hear. The other three watched the can swell, then moved away when it was about to break and spew hot tomato juice over whoever happened to be near. Once a particularly strong tin held until it burst with a noise like a pistol shot. Nobody spoke except Step, who observed in his gentle voice, "Anatole, why are you such a *noisy* cook?"

Still Anatole could not remember to puncture the tin before he placed it on the fire. Step and Walter were too stubborn, or perhaps too amused, to puncture it for him. Delore had never seen a trail boss take part in cooking, so he, too, refrained from helping Anatole, and their meals continued to be frequently punctuated by the sound of bursting tomato tins.

Anatole also had difficulty in distinguishing coffee from tea. The method of cooking was the same for both. Into a blackened lard pail he would pour cold water and a handful of tea (or coffee). The pail would be hung over the centre of the campfire and, after boiling vigorously for a time, drunk. Both tea and coffee became so black by this method that it was a little difficult to distinguish between the two, but as Step would say, "There is some small, some delicate difference between tea and coffee for us conoseers, Anatole."

Each night and morning, Anatole would ask which brew they preferred. Each time, no matter what their answer, he threw in a handful of material from the first tin that came to his hand.

"Any time you get tired of cowboying," Step would say, "there is a great future for you as top cook at the Ritzey Plaza in Vancouver." Anatole would smile. He never seemed to resent Step's teasing.

After Anatole had been obliged to shift to the blue roan packhorse for a saddle horse, having worn his own horse down, he encountered new troubles. The blue roan had been running free on Frenchie's range for four straight years. It hated being packed and it hated even more being obliged to carry a man. Accordingly it greeted each day in a foul mood. Anatole had little difficulty, usually, in catching the roan on the meadows, chasing after the hobbled horse as it humped across the grass, grabbing it by the mane, then wrapping his arm about the ugly ewe-neck and dragging the bit into its mouth. The blue would also allow himself to be saddled without doing anything more provocative than expanding his belly and holding his breath, so that it was impossible to get the cinch tight enough unless he was kneed in the guts and obliged to exhale. Anatole could never remember to do this, and usually his saddle began to slip sideways five minutes from camp. He would have to dismount and try again to tighten the cinch, whereupon the blue would again puff himself up so it could not be made tight enough.

But this was not all. The blue preferred to start each day with violent exercise. The first morning and the second morning, and the third and fourth, too, Step would make his mild suggestion to Anatole just as the latter was about to mount.

"I really think it might be best if you walk him around for a minute or two and unwind that horse," he would say, "I think it might take some of the kink out of his backbone."

Walter usually did this with his own horse. Delore had done so also with Stella, when she was newly broken. Walking a horse in a little circle before mounting did indeed seem to take the kink out of the backbone. But Anatole could never remember. Each day he would step straight into the saddle. "As if he was getting on a streetcar," Step would say.

Three times, so far, the blue had put down his head and bucked and Anatole had come off on the ground in a tangle of arms and legs. Once it looked as though he had fallen on his head and Delore was afraid Anatole had broken his neck, but Anatole had got to his feet with only a little blood running down his face from a cut above his right eye. He had shaken his head a few times, some drops of blood flew from the point of his chin, and then he had smiled in the usual way and got aboard the blue again.

"I do believe, Anatole, that your future is in the Ritzey Plaza," Step would say.

Step was almost always calm. The only exception

was when he began to talk about liquor and religion. Then his voice became harsh, almost strident, and he would talk about being washed in the Blood of the Lamb and curse quite foully about people who were not. Walter coaxed him into these spasms of anger a couple of times before Step realized he was being teased. Thereafter Step was silent on the subject, except when he and Delore found themselves alone and out of earshot of the others, at which times Step would whisper, "I tell you, kid, never trust the Indians with liquor. It don't act on them like a white man. Remember that. One ounce . . ."—he would hold rough thumb and forefinger an inch apart—". . . *one ounce* . . . and they're away. They can't handle their liquor."

Generally, however, Step was the calmest man that Delore had ever seen, and he was never calmer than the day Anatole shot the chicken.

One of Anatole's few possessions was a slip of paper, creased and torn, limp as cloth, scrawled with the X that was his signature, which declared him to be a licensed prospector. It was called, for reasons unknown to Delore, a Free Miner's Licence, although he knew it cost five dollars. How or why Anatole had acquired his he did not know, and he could not seem to get it through Anatole's bushy head that the licence was good only for one year. Anatole thought he was licensed for life, and nothing could shake his belief. One of the privileges of a free miner was that he might carry a pistol so that he could obtain food for himself "when in actual need."

Anatole had found no claims to stake but he had

acquired a pistol. It was an old Stevens .22 calibre single-shot, shaped like a revolver, but having only an imitation of the revolving chamber. It was a small thing and Anatole kept it in the right-hand pocket of his blue jeans where it had polished itself to a silver-white. For some reason someone had at one time taken a hacksaw to the barrel of the pistol and shortened it to about three inches, soldering on a half-dime as a replacement for the front sight. It was a useless sort of gun but Anatole liked it. He slept with it beneath his pillow each night, tucked it into his pants pocket each morning, and frequently through the course of each day would say, "Too bad, I don't see no chicken."

The grouse, which were called chicken by all ranchers and cowboys in the Namko country, were scarce this year. Having been so plentiful the previous year that Delore had become tired of eating them, they now seemed to have vanished from the face of the earth. This happened about every seven years or so. Nobody knew why.

It was on the eighth day out from the Long Opening, where the drive had started. Walter was ahead, walking the drive east into the sun, which now stood four fingers' breadth, one hour, above the horizon. Step and Delore had stayed behind with the train to watch Anatole climb the second time, as usual, into the saddle of the blue roan. Now they walked away from the cold camp on the trail which had been beaten to dust by the feet of one hundred and ninety-six cattle a few minutes before. Anatole led the black mare, first of the pack train. The other five packhorses followed— the strange Appaloosa, three bays and finally Anatole's sore-backed saddle horse. The pack train was no longer roped nose to tail. Like the cattle in the drive, they were now resigned to following the long trail east. They had, apparently, forgotten the home meadows of Namko. Delore and Step were just riding to take up their positions when suddenly Anatole flung up his arm. All stopped.

"Chicken!" said Anatole, "Chicken! Chicken! Chicken! Chicken!" He was flinging himself off the blue roan even as he said the words, tugging at his pants pocket to free the pistol.

Delore was puzzled by Anatole's excitement. What did a little chicken amount to? They needed a deer, not that poor scrawny little fool-hen which he could distinguish sitting, typically stupid, upon a deadfall just ahead of the first horse.

Step cleared his throat and said, "Anatole, I really do think . . ." But the little pistol barked before he could finish.

Anatole had held the gun just beside his saddle horse. The blue had stood many times while rifles had been fired near his little pin ears, but he had never seen flame fly from the end of a man's fingers, nor heard so sharp and unpleasant a *pop* in his ear as the snub-nosed pistol made. He broke up the trail at a full gallop, stepping on one rein and breaking it as he went. The black mare, next in line, reared, pawed the air, narrowly missed pulling off one of Anatole's ears as she came down, and raced into the thick jack pine beside the trail. The Appaloosa followed. Step spurred toward the three bay packhorses, but not soon enough. They went the opposite way. Anatole's old mare, last of the

train, spun and went down the way they had come.
Delore tried to put his horse in front of her to stop her
run but could not move Stella fast enough. He ran
Stella down the trail after her. All about was the pop-
ping and crashing of timber as the pack train scattered.

Delore headed off Anatole's mare and brought her to
a stop but she broke away from him when the black
mare thundered past them, Step riding close behind.
When the black veered off into the trees Step followed.
The mare brushed against a pine. There was a crackl-
ing of broken pack box. Splinters flew. Tinned tomatoes rolled out.

Step spurred up behind her but saw, too late, a heavy
tree limb stretched across his face. He threw up his arm
to protect himself but the horse kept running beneath
him. Step was lifted out of the saddle, his legs slid
back along the horse's flanks. He held the tree limb
as long as he could but the effect was only to rake his
own horse all the harder with the spurs, and in one fast
jump the horse was gone and Step had landed. The
old cowboy hit the ground like a falling tree, heels first,
then, still stiff, the rest of him, his hat flying off, the fine
duff of the forest floor puffing up around him.

"You all right, Step?"

"It's them horses ain't all right. Get that mare. She's
the craziest one of all." Step rolled over, brushed himself off, and began an awkward step-and-a-skip run
after his own horse which now stood, looking a little
foolish itself, about twenty feet away.

Abandoning all hope of catching Anatole's horse,
Delore rode after the black mare, following her by the
sound of crashing trees, noting spilled beans and

tomato cans under the trees as he went. Branches whipped his hat and tore at his sleeves. Stella was panting. The packhorse ran full tilt into a two-foot-thick fir, staggered a moment and fell to the ground, cracking the pack box on the other side as she fell. *She must be the stupidest horse in the world,* thought Delore, as he jumped off and grabbed her halter. She thrashed her legs a few times, rolled over, splitting some more wood from the pack box, and got to her feet. Delore tied her securely to a jack pine. By the time he left she was trying to graze. That was a horse for you.

Delore went back to the scene of the chicken shooting.

One of the bays had rolled on its back to break up its pack. When it rose, the pack had slipped back toward the loin. The horse reacted like a rodeo bronc and the sky was filled with feet, snorts and cracking timbers.

Step rode up, swinging his rope. He dropped it neatly over the neck of the bucking horse. Delore, in two tries, got his rope on. They walked their horses opposite ways; the packhorse, finding himself held, decided that the moment for calm and reflection had come and stood, shivering, wet with sweat, while they tied their ropes to nearby trees and then came to him to free him of the broken pack.

"Always a sale for this horse at Calgary Stampede," said Step.

The Appaloosa had stood among the timber until now. Step walked ahead to tie it. The Appaloosa, however, began to walk, dragging him at the end of the halter rope. Step flung his arms about the horse's neck and grabbed an ear in his teeth. This should have halted any horse, but still the Appaloosa walked a few more steps, scraping the grunting old cowboy against the pines as it went and ripping the back out of his shirt.

Step had just finally brought it to a halt when Anatole came out of the nearby deadfalls, leading another packhorse.

"I don't see that old mare I got," he said, as he tied it to a tree.

Step, although panting from his battle with the Appaloosa, kept his voice low and even. "She's just over there," he said, pointing down the trail.

"I don't see her," said Anatole.

"Just over there," said Step, pointing again. "Just seventy-five miles down that way toward Namko. If you hurry you can catch that horse before the week is out."

"I don't know what I do now."

"My suggestion would be," said Step, "that you hurry."

Anatole galloped down the trail on the blue roan, riding all over his horse as usual, appearing to stay aboard more by coincidence than skill. It was three hours before he returned with the lost mare. Meanwhile Delore and Step had rebuilt the broken packs as best they could and retrieved what beans, bacon and canned tomatoes they could find in the timber. They were waiting with the pack train when Anatole rode up.

Just as they were about to leave, Step spoke to Anatole.

"There is one thing I would like to ask you," he said, ". . . if you don't mind."

Anatole waited.

Step said, "Did you hit that bloody little bird that you was shooting at?"

Anatole gave a weak smile. "I guess I did," he said. "But when all them horses untracked themselfs I just threw him away."

Step dismounted and tied his horse.

"I think," he said, "we will just find that bird. By my estimation, that bird has cost us about forty-seven dollars, which must work out to about seventy-five dollars to the pound, dressed weight. It will be the finest meat you have ever eaten in all the Cariboo country."

After a ten-minute search they found the dead chicken. Step tied it by the feet and hung it carefully on Anatole's saddle horn. That night at camp Step stood over Anatole while he cooked the chicken. Anatole did not cook even beans very well, and the chicken he fried was as hard and tasteless as jerked beef.

The piece on Step's plate was not much bigger than would be provided by a sparrow, but Step picked the tiny bones clean. The only thing he said was, "Funny thing, ain't it? This don't taste no better than any other chicken I've ate in this country."

HIGH WATER ON THE UGULKUTZ

Next day they rode into the long wide valley that led down from the Stack. The Stack was the black core of a volcano that had raged here many millions of years ago, the geologists said. Lightning and fire and flame and poisonous gases must have covered all this land. Thousands of miles of the face of the earth must have been torn into black and red horror by the Stack, but it was hard to imagine so now. True, there were still, among the tufted hummocks of grass, spongelike pieces of black and red lava rock, but the twenty miles between the Namko beef drive and the Stack were now gentle slopes of pine and poplar and meadow. Flowers still spattered the grass beside the occasional boulders; the wind was warm and the sun was hot.

Delore was riding beside Step. He often did, now. Step was like the Stack: an old volcano, with all its violence spent; rough, lined with the cracks of age, but softened also by the slow wash of time. He felt more secure when he rode with Step-and-a-Half Jones. He wondered again why Frenchie had not ordered Step to take in the drive. What his father actually said was, "Use Step. *But not too much.*" Why?

Some sharptails flushed near the pack train but Anatole left his pistol in his pocket.

"Anatole is letting those chickens go now," said Delore.

"Yeah."

"I guess he learned something, Step."

"Mp hmmp." Step spat tobacco juice past his horse's ear.

"He ain't very smart, is he?" Step looked but said nothing, so Delore continued, "After all, why go to trouble for just one chicken?"

"Well," said Step, very slowly, "I would spose you have never been as hungry as Anatole in your life." While Delore was digesting this, Step continued, "Maybe we had better go upstream some before we try to cross the Ugulkutz."

"What is there to crossing the Ugulkutz?" said Delore. "It's only a little creek."

Step looked toward the Stack. All through the morning there had been black cloud above the Stack and occasional streaks of sheet lightning. Much of the time they could see the grey curtain of rain reaching down to one side or the other of the mountain. Once a heavy black cloud had shut out the sun over the drive, and hail the size of large green peas had pounded their hats and their horses and bounced high on the grass about them.

"She'll be booming up high," said Step.

"There's a good ford just ahead," said Delore. He indicated with a nod of the tip of his hat a patch of high poplar about a mile ahead. There, unless his memory of previous drives was failing him, the

Ugulkutz rippled across a gravel bar and the water was less than a foot deep. Cattle might balk at the edge but it was not difficult to coax them onto the bar and, once the first had waded across, blowing foam from her nose and raising foam with her heels, the rest would follow. Frenchie told of being forced to swim his drive on the Ugulkutz once but Delore had never seen the river so high, nor had he ever heard of any other drives swimming on the pretty little river that came down the broad valley from the Stack.

"That takes us the wrong way," said Step.

"It ain't out of our way. We cut from there straight across to Bald Hill Lake," said Delore, pointing to a patch of yellow grass that lay, high on a ridge beside a hidden lake, not far below the eastern horizon. With any luck, they would camp on Bald Hill tonight.

"That's the lower trail," said Step.

Delore stopped his horse. So did Step.

"Step, what's all this business about? You and Walter and Anatole have been talking about the lower trail and the high trail through here ever since we left Namko."

"I figured I told you, half a dozen times."

"Well, you didn't."

"The low trail goes past Sitkum Casmeer's place."

"I know that."

"And Sitkum Casmeer makes hooch."

"Frenchie and me have gone through Sitkum's and there wasn't any liquor around."

"Frenchie don't drink, not when he's bossing a drive, anyhow."

"How do you know Anatole or Walter drink?" Step

did not answer and Delore continued, "I heard Walter ask you if you ever saw him drunk. First day out, it was. You never answered."

"Indians can't stand the booze. One sniff of the cork . . ."

"But you never answered Walter. Why do you say he drinks? Have you ever seen Walter drunk? I haven't."

Step said, "Never trust Siwashes near booze, I tell ya."

"Don't call them Siwashes!"

Step spat again and rode ahead. "We'll take the upper side," he said, pointing a few miles upstream to another ridge of grass that bent northward, far from Sitkum Casmeer's cabin.

"We will go across here," said Delore, keeping his voice as loud and even as he could. Step stopped, straightened his back, looked at the ridges on the other side of the Ugulkutz and did not answer.

Delore rode past him and called ahead to Walter who rode not far ahead, "Walter!" Delore paused, his right arm out high. "We go at the old crossing!"

He could not see if Walter smiled but he saw Walter move quickly; first to Anatole, to direct the pack train toward the Ugulkutz ford; then back, yipping gently, "Hiyu, hiyu, yu yu." Walter turned the drive down.

When Delore reached the banks of the Ugulkutz he realized that Step had been right, as Step so often was.

The little creek was high, rust brown in colour, oily and ugly. Small tree roots and branches rose and sank in its boils as it cut past the bank with a sound of *slurp, slurp, slurp*. From somewhere came a long, sucking noise. He saw the source, a few yards distant. The current was eating out the roots of a pine tree at the bank. As he watched, the pine slowly drifted into the water. Foam built around its green branches. Rocks clattered down the steep bank as more tendrils of root tore free. There was a boil, a scouring rush of water, and the twenty-foot pine tree left the bank and dipped into the dirty water. High trail or low trail, they should have taken the upper crossing, as Step had suggested, up where the Ugulkutz broke into two parts and where each half of the stream could be expected to be only half so fierce and strong as here at the main fording place.

The cattle bawled and backed from the waters.

Behind a ridge of tall alder in the swampy meadow he saw Walter moving fast to bunch them tighter on the bank beside the ford.

Anatole had tied the packhorses farther up the dry hill that led down to the creek. Now Anatole, too, rode down, faster than he usually rode, and pushed more cattle into the narrow patch of grass at the edge of the ford.

The Indians were not helping by doing this. The drive should be allowed to fan out along the river bank, to give the animals time to get used to the sight and sound of the fast water. Then it would be possible to get the lead cow into the stream, then a few more after her, and finally all the drive would follow the leader to the opposite bank for no other reason than that they did not want to be left alone. Once a drive began to move, nothing would stop them. But the beef drive was piling up in the little quarter-mile-long flat beside the ford, and there was a note of panic in their bawling. Cows clambered up over the backs of other cows. A yearling, Delore noticed, was being crushed by bigger animals about it as a whirlpool began to form in the herd—a whirlpool not unlike the swirl of dirty red water forming beside the bank of the river.

"Don't push them," Delore called to the two Indian cowboys, but the bawling of the cattle and the heavy roar of the river drowned his voice.

At any minute the drive would break, probably up or down the river bank, spilling weaker animals into the river as it surged along the banks. Delore's only thought was, *How many do I have to lose? Can I get by with losing five? With losing eight?*

Hadn't somebody once lost half his drive in the Whitewater River to the south? Yes, somebody had. So the story went. Red and white carcasses, rotting on the gravel banks for months afterward.

"We'll take the upper ford," he called to Step. But Step, if he heard, did not answer.

A swirl of the herd came toward him. Near the edge he saw the old cow which had led the drive for the past seven days. She was bawling, too, but there was something different about the way she carried her head. Delore looked closely at her. Yes, that was it. Alone among all the frightened steers with which she mixed, the old cow had her eyes on the opposite bank of the river.

Perhaps, with speed and luck. . . .

With his right hand Delore pulled out his rope from where it hung at the fork of his saddle, with his left he shook out the noose. Stella forced her way through bawling cattle to the old cow on the river bank. Delore settled the noose easily over the old cow's head, dallied his rope to the saddle horn. He held the cow up beside Stella on a very short rope.

Then he touched Stella with his spurs and also slapped her once, quickly, on the rump with the end of his reins. Knotted together, man, horse and cow lurched down the slippery bank together and into the boil of the river.

As he slipped out of the saddle, gasping when he hit the cold water, Delore loosed the dally from his saddle horn. Stella was free to swim to the opposite bank and, with luck, the cow and the rest of the drive would follow them. Stella was not a horse that swam well. She carried herself very low in the water, which she hated and feared. Delore floated beside her, one hand twisted in her mane. He felt his heavy chaps drag him down. The current was far faster than he had realized. They were being carried rapidly downstream, and when he cleared the water from his eyes the opposite bank seemed to be spinning away from them. He looked behind. The cow was following. But a rope was coming toward him. Anatole, his mouth open as though he were shouting, was trying to rope him. The noose settled over Delore's head and began to pull tight. Panicked by the thought of strangling on a rope's end, he took both hands to claw it away from him. He freed it from his head but it tightened hard on one wrist and, pendulum-like, carried by the current, he was swept away from Stella, past the snorting cow and under the water.

Roaring water beat up his nose. He must not swallow

or try to breathe. He was sinking, then rising. His face burst out of the foam again. Gasping, choking, he had one instant to look back along the rope which held him to Anatole's horse. The saddle was empty. The horse was braced against the pull of the rope, as a good horse should be, and very efficiently drowning him in a whirlpool of the Ugulkutz. As he went under again he could only wonder whether Walter and Step would be able to force their way through the bawling herd soon enough to loose the rope and let him swim to safety.

Then he was telling himself again, *Don't breathe, don't try to breathe,* while the water roared in his eardrums, and a clamp of pain settled on his chest and yellow and green lights began to show behind his closed eyelids.

Then there was no more tension on his wrist. Someone had loosed the rope.

Now Delore went downstream with the boiling river, turning a complete somersault in the water first, then seeing daylight, gulping air so hard that it burned his throat, filling his lungs before he rolled under the surface again. There was a louder roar, and something rough against his side. He surfaced again. He was tangled in the arms of the jack pine, which had broken free of the bank just minutes before. The jack pine was jammed against a snag on the river bank and he was jammed in the jack pine. The jack pine dipped below the surface, and Delore went under again.

He held his breath. *How long, how long this time?*

A strong hand grabbed his wrist and pulled him higher up the trunk, free of the water. He looked into

Walter's face. The cowboy had come down the trunk from the bank. Now, with surprising strength, he dragged Delore up the rough trunk, scraping his face on the sharp branches.

"You hold on good," said Walter. "I try for Anatole." He crawled over Delore's body into the deeper water that covered the end of the pine. Water beat upon him.

"Where's Anatole?" said Delore.

Walter's voice came back above the roar of the river. "He jumps in after you."

The tree sank lower. The river, with more leverage to exert, tore more of its roots from the bank and it now swung almost parallel to the shore, its top downstream. Delore jumped to the bank, turned, saw Walter struggling with the body of Anatole where the thick branches lay in the water. So Anatole, too, had hung up in the tree.

From the bank above, Step threw his rope. Walter caught it, wound it about Anatole's chest and, helped by Step's backing horse, they brought Anatole through shallow water and onto the gravel bank beside Delore.

Anatole had apparently succeeded in keeping his face above water. He vomited out only a little, wheezed and coughed for a moment, then lay face down, trembling, upon the gravel bank.

"Damn fool," came Step's voice from the bank above. "First he panics and ropes you off your horse. Then he ain't got enough sense to either let you free or to pull you in. He just jumps into the water beside you and goes down like a stone."

Walter, unspeaking, climbed up the cut bank to his horse.

"We'll just sit here a while," said Delore.

Upstream, he saw, the rest of the drive had followed the cow as he had hoped, and all were making their way quite well to the opposite bank. Most of the river was very shallow, after all. The whole episode had taken place in one small, deep hole against this bank. What a stupid way it would have been to die. And all because of Anatole. The cowboy still lay beside him on the gravel, his face, grey with fright, pressed to the grey rocks, his back heaving as he drew fresh air to his lungs, his chunky body shivering. Delore loosed the rope from his wrist. His hand, he noticed, was dark with congested blood. Anatole, watching this, said, "Ain't smart what I do, I guess."

"It's okay. We're out of it. We'll swim across with the packhorses."

"Better I drag you out," said Anatole, "but I don't think. I just jump in to grab you. Sure no good, cause I don't know how to swim."

"You can't swim!"

Anatole turned his face away. "Ain't very smart in the head," he said.

"You can't swim, and you jumped into that to get me out?"

There was no answer. Delore put a hand on Anatole's shoulder and said, "Thanks, Anatole. You're a brave man." But the cowboy just shivered, and after a few moments Delore, thoughtful, went up the bank to see the last of the cattle cross the river.

He thought some more about Anatole's desperate

jump into the flood when he watched him go, again rigid with fright, half out of the water on the withers of the hard-swimming roan. Anatole must have overcome a paralyzing fear of water to have thrown himself into the river in his mixed-up attempt at a rescue.

That night Delore announced, positively, that the drive would take the lower trail, and not all the loud and tiresome argument of Step-and-a-Half Jones could prevail against him.

SITKUM'S

Three days later Delore knew that he should have taken Step's advice.

They had ridden past the old cabin where lived Sitkum Casmeer the day after passing the Ugulkutz. The cabin had been built some forty or fifty years ago and was tucked into a sidehill, only a few of the logs protruding past the thin-sodded slope of the grassland. The roof was of sod also and had grown hay, almost a foot high, during the summer. A rusty stovepipe poked out through the ground where the cabin was thrust deep into the sidehill, and a wisp of blue smoke was lifting from it as they neared.

Sitkum came to the door as they passed. He was an old bent man. White, Indian or half-and-half? Delore could not tell. He would have ridden up to the soddy and talked with Sitkum. It had been now almost eighteen days since he had spoken with any man except the three cowboys of the Namko drive and Stetler. He noticed, however, that the cowboys paid little attention to Sitkum as they rode past. Anatole waved, once. Walter, using the old Chinook dialect said softly, "Klahowya, Sitkum." Step-and-a-Half Jones had kept his eyes straight ahead until almost beside Sitkum's door. Then he had turned, nodded curtly, once, and returned his eyes to the beef drive.

So Delore also had walked his mare quietly past and when opposite the door, where he saw Sitkum Casmeer's white head, he lifted a hand and said, "Hi," flat-voiced, and rode on.

That night they camped a mile past Sitkum's. Step wanted to go further, but already it was almost dark and normally they began to make camp for the night a full two hours before darkness fell.

"We stay on this Holding Ground, it's more better," Walter had said.

The Holding Ground, as it turned out, was not complete. Two drift fences ran from the edge of the Nine Mile Creek across the wide, rich meadows of grass, three miles to the timber. They were a familiar type of fencing, the Russel fence. Triangles of poles held three dangling poles, looped in rust-red fencing wire, to each section. But they were only drift fences. They ran from the creek, which was so heavy in willow that probably cows would not bother to thrust through it, up to the jack pine ridge a thousand feet higher on the grassland. Then the drift fences trailed away into the timber and ended, in the expectation that cattle would prefer the open grass to the sparse, turpentine-flavoured grass that grew beneath the pines.

Delore insisted they ride night herd. He had already lost one steer to thin-lipped old Stetler, being left instead with the stringy old cow that looked, as Step said, old enough to vote.

Anatole disappeared the first night. He returned

next morning, demanding "something to drink" and, on being told to work instead, had lurched off, clambered on the blue roan bareback and ridden madly away into the pearly dawn.

"He rides better drunk," observed Step.

Step cooked breakfast that first morning, while Delore wondered whether it might not be better to go on without Anatole. Three men could, he supposed, handle the drive. Before he could make up his mind, Step rode down toward Sitkum's to collect Anatole, as he put it. Step was gone for hours. By the time he returned, without Anatole, Walter had left.

Walter rode off in the direction of Sitkum's cabin. Delore saw him go when he came back from the creek with a bucket of water for the midday meal. There were two horses, he saw, moving into the trees at the sky line.

So Walter was taking away the Appaloosa packhorse. Not once, since that packhorse joined the train, had its boxes been opened. Each night Walter had unpacked the Appaloosa and set the tightly tied boxes beside a tree at the camp site.

Well, good enough. If they were for Sitkum Casmeer, at least they were delivered. And if they contained liquor, at least Walter had not opened them during the drive.

Step maintained that Sitkum had no interest in anything except what he called "dirty, rotten, stinking drink." Perhaps that was why he had ridden so stone-faced past Sitkum's old cabin.

I don't care, thought Delore, *what he's delivering or how he does it. All I want to do is move one hundred and ninety-six head of stock to Williams Lake.* But he gave up all thought of moving the beef drive that day.

He expected Walter back at sundown. Walter did not come. Neither did Anatole.

Just as the shadows of the ridge ate their way across the grass to the alder clumps by the river, Step rode back after a second visit to Sitkum's.

"Make up your mind for it, kid," he said, "they've got to drink their way through that booze before we move."

Delore was lighting feather sticks to start the evening fire.

"It ain't so bad," said Step, "we're two days ahead on this drive."

"We are?"

"Well, by last year's drive, sure."

"D'you figure we should just sit here and wait until they feel like coming back, Step?"

Step spread his hands before the thin flame of the first three feather sticks. "There ain't no choice," he said.

That second night, Step-and-a-Half rode herd until midnight. Delore rode until six in the morning. Both slept in the warmth of the early morning, when the sun took charge of the Namko drive. At noon of the third day, while they ate bacon that was beginning to taste just a little rancid, Delore said, "What should I do, Step?"

Step chewed the lean meat of the bacon, which was all he chose to eat that day, and then said, "My advice is, never interfere with a man when he's drinking."

"You were against coming this way because they might start drinking. I wish I'd listened to you."

"Never," repeated Step, "interfere with a man when he's drinking." He stood and brushed his mouth, leaving a faintly shining streak across the white whiskers at the side of his face.

This was the first day that Step had not shaved. *He must be as tired as I am*, thought Delore. Two men were not enough for this job on a half-fenced patch of these long, open grasslands near the Fraser.

"I sure should have taken your advice, Step," said Delore.

"What's done is done," said Step. He tugged at the bandana that was wound around his neck, tightened the knot near his prominent Adam's apple and said, "I'll keep an eye on the cattle until about midnight. Then you take over again."

Delore was not sleepy, but when he lay down the heat of the sun seemed to press him gently into the ground and a warm wash of sleep drowned all his worries. Later that afternoon he awakened when Anatole Harry lurched into the camp. Anatole was obviously drunk. The metal buttons of his denim jacket were all undone. His hair was over his eyes. He had no hat. Delore watched him through the shade of his eyelashes. Nothing was to be gained by revealing that he was awake.

Step walked into view and put a hand on Anatole's shoulder. It was strange to Delore. He had never before seen Step touch any man with his hand.

"Damn stinking booze," said Step.

Anatole looked at him and smiled. Anatole always

smiled, even when drunk. There was more conversation, which Delore could not hear. Then Anatole left. When he woke again, it was dark. He could not see Step. The waning moon lit the big meadow only dimly.

He dressed, made a fire, cooked scalding hot coffee and burnt his mouth on it.

While he waited by the fire for Step, all the thoughts that he had pushed away with sleep came rushing back to him, shrill, yammering, nagging questions:

Why was the extra packhorse in this outfit? Why had Walter always kept the pack boxes shut so tight? What was in them? And why didn't you look, eh? Why didn't you look?

When would Anatole be sober again? How drunk is Walter? What is there about that brand on the Appaloosa?

This is a one-night Holding Ground, Delore Bernard, and you're in your third day on it already. What if someone reports you? How much is the fine? Who pays it?

Silly Delore. Silly boy. Silly boy.

The coffee was cold, and he'd drunk only one mouthful. He poured it on the ground. He was not hungry. Maybe he'd eat just before taking over from Step at midnight. He walked across the meadow to where Stella grazed and pulled himself carefully up on her back. "Let's take a walk, Stella," he whispered. Not bothering with the bridle, he guided her with her halter rope.

Placing her feet softly as she moved, because she seemed to sense his mood, Stella carried him easily, slowly, toward Sitkum Casmeer's cabin, through the patches of cattle, past the still white waters of a little lake. The stars were close and burning brightly, the moon was low on the western hills. He could not see Step. The old cowboy probably was walking his horse through the solid blackness that lay beneath the jack pine, high on the ridge. If Step saw him, he would probably ride down and warn him again that there was no point in interfering with a man while he was drinking. He knew that. But he wanted to see what went on at Casmeer's soddy in the sidehill. He lay low on Stella's neck. Perhaps in the distance, Step would not see him; Stella would be just another horse, ambling through the drive.

The square bulk of Casmeer's grew out of the deep shadow of the sidehill. He stopped, and they watched. The dim bulk of a horse stirred beside the long overhang of the roof at the front of the cabin. Was it one horse, or two?

Why any horses, tied at the cabin door? Walter would have turned loose the Appaloosa after unpacking the liquor for Casmeer. His own saddle horse he would have also turned loose to graze inside Casmeer's fencing. Anatole, in his condition, would scarcely remember to tie his horse.

Two blobs of darkness detached themselves from the shadow of the cabin and moved across the meadow, one behind the other.

The moon was almost down. Blackness ate up the pale grass of the meadow.

He crouched lower on Stella's neck and walked her toward the two shapes. Stella walked very softly. He heard one of the horses in front step on a loose piece of rock. It was louder than the sound of his own horse's feet on the sod. Delore walked her diagonally to the line he expected the two other animals to walk and waited under the umbrella of a poplar, silent and un-whispering now because there was not enough wind to stir its leaves. That was good, what drift of air existed came to his face. The other animals would not smell Stella.

Delore slipped off his horse, one hand holding her halter rope, the other held at her nostrils to signal her not to whinny. Stella would catch the scent of the others as they passed.

The dim shapes of the other two horses grew to their left. Stella shook her head. He held her tighter.

Only five or ten feet from them, it seemed, the two horses passed, and against the pale grass Delore could now clearly distinguish them. There was a man on the lead horse. The second had a square shape to its back.

Walter was leading the Appaloosa away from Cas-meer's, and the Appaloosa was packed again and, judging by its gait, the pack was heavy still. Delore climbed back on Stella and gently, following the other two horses through the poplar and the pines by sound and sometimes by sight, he followed the mysterious Walter and the mysterious outlaw horse into the full blackness of the pine forest.

MATHOOSE

Fifteen minutes from the meadow, as they were passing through a grove of the heavy, orange-barked fir,
the blast of a whinny came from one of the horses
ahead. Delore could not reach Stella's nostrils to stop
her answering so he reached up her neck to her ear, and
twisted it. It confused Stella. This was no signal that
she knew, but in her confusion she stopped short of
replying to the horse in front of her. All three animals
stood. Walter did not speak. A coyote yelped ahead
of them in the dark timber, not the quavering orchestra
that coyotes make when they stand at the edge of a
ravine and make echoes bounce back and forth against
their own voices, but a short, sharp bark.

Walter and his packhorse moved away, at a trot for
the first time.

Delore trotted Stella after them, but now the sound
of her feet on the brittle deadwood beneath the trees
was louder than the sounds made by the other horses.
Within a minute or two, he had lost the others. He
stopped Stella and listened. The coyote yelped again
and another answered not far ahead of him, just to the
left. But of the other horses there was no sign at all.

Whatever Walter's errand with that extra packhorse, he would not discover it tonight.

Delore walked Stella through the timber a few minutes more. The coyotes were silent, and now the moon was down and the night was deeper than ever.

Only the stars shone, and they seemed much brighter than before. One ahead, particularly, glowed like a kerosene lantern. Would it be Venus, the morning star? Already?

He walked the horse toward it. It was not a star, it was a campfire. Delore slipped off Stella's back again, tied her to a small tree and walked toward the fire, placing the balls of his feet on the ground first, feeling as he placed them for the springy touch of dry sticks that might snap. It must be a very, very small fire. Indians usually made small fires, but this was a tiny thing. If it had winked out, it would be possible to believe he had seen the match flare of a man lighting a cigarette. Delore edged closer, passing from the shade of one big fir tree to another.

"Hello, boss," said Walter, very softly.

Walter had halted his horses, got off, and had stood there, holding the lead horse and waiting for Delore to walk up beside him.

There was nothing to say.

"You come visit us at this campfire, eh, boss," said Walter. Walter spoke very softly, almost a whisper.

"Just looking around," said Delore.

"You come so far," said Walter, "better, I guess, you come right down this campfire." Walter walked his saddle horse closer and said, "You come right down this place, boss. Spose you're here, I guess you come this camp."

"Sure. Okay."

They walked together toward the little fire. It was not much larger than a dinner plate. It was being fed with sticks the size of pencils by a figure dimly seen in the wavering, yellow flame.

"Hello this place!" said Walter, giving the usual greeting to announce entry to a camp, but the figure did not look up. Walter tied his horses to a tree and, together with Delore, walked into the little pool of yellow firelight and squatted on his heels. Walter contributed a stick to the fire, which seized it with a faint crackle.

His voice was cold as thin ice at the edge of a pond when he said, "The boss of this drive, he comes with me for a visit."

The figure at the fire did not look up.

Delore kept his eyes carefully focused on the flame wrapping around the new stick of the fire. Walter half turned toward him. "This is my friend," he said.

The friend did not acknowledge the words. Neither did Delore. Delore continued to look into the little fire. A drop of sweat formed between his shoulder blades and traced a cold trail down his back to his tail bone. He did not need to be told who this man was. Now he knew why this hidden fire was lit in the timber, why the extra packhorse, why Walter had brought it away, secretly, from Sitkum Casmeer's.

The man at the fire was Mathoose.

THE LONG, LONG CONVERSATION

For as many years as he could remember Delore had known of Mathoose, the murderer. The killing had taken place on an Indian Reserve when Delore was very small. It was possible that it happened before he was born, although he seemed to have a dim recollection of his mother and father discussing it in very quiet voices one bitter night, many years ago, when the frost was building up on the inside walls of their log-cabin ranch house, his father saying, "Two men, shot in the back, just for the fun of it . . ." and his mother saying softly, "Be quiet. You will wake the children."

But this, perhaps, was another time, the time one of his father's best horses was stolen. It was never found, but when the B.C. Provincial Policeman had driven up to talk to his father about the horse he had heard, again, the name Mathoose.

When Delore was about ten years old, an eighty-year-old trapper was found shot to death in his cabin on the Tappan Mountain, and for three days there had been policemen at Frenchie's ranch; two of them, with a tracker, following a trail across the mountain until they lost it, the third bringing in the trapper's body strapped on a packhorse. His father said afterward that the old man had shot himself, having lost his mind living alone so long under the swish of the Northern Lights, which had filled the sky so long that winter. Others in Namko, however, said that it was Mathoose who had killed the trapper, and Delore remembered that his younger brother, Hector, had nightmares, night after night, week after week, that long winter of the bright Northern Lights. His mother would have to come to the boys' bedroom in the flaring and fading glow from the north, her long hair unbound and falling to her waist, and she would sleep with little Hector and say, "Mathoose cannot get you, little Hector, you are safe in our house."

Now he, Delore, sat across a small fire in the deep and lonely fir forest and on the other side was the man he knew to be Mathoose. And Walter, he knew, had come on the beef drive for one purpose only: to bring a supply of food to the murderer. There was a gun beside Mathoose on the ground, a .30-.30 Winchester. He could see the light of the fire on its barrel without looking directly toward it.

"I guess there ain't no cattle up this far," said Delore.

"Sure guess there ain't, boss."

"Well," Delore stood up and stretched. He could feel his knees shake. "I guess I might as well go along."

"I think it's better you just stay this place, boss."

Delore squatted again beside the fire.

"You don't know this friend I got."

Delore tried to speak softly, calmly, as Walter did. "I only know I got one hundred and ninety-six cattle to get to Williams Lake, Walter."

He looked at Walter, hoping to see some softening

in that lean, dark face, but Walter's face was stiff and cold.

"You don't know that man. Sure funny, ain't it?"

Delore looked at the fire.

"Might be better, spose you look at that man, real good," said Walter.

Delore's head turned stiffly. He did not want it to but it turned, and he looked at the man whom no white in the Namko country was known to have looked upon for many, many years.

He looked first at the man's feet. They were in moccasins black with age. Thick, sewn of untanned moose hide, nevertheless they were worn through at the toe and split on one side. Above the moccasins, two thin ankles, skin stretched tight over a jumble of bones and tendons. A torn pair of blue suit pants. (Blue serge! From where? From Walter's supply last fall? If so, where did Walter obtain suit pants? From a second-hand store at Williams Lake, perhaps?)

Mathoose wore a sweater, ravelled at the cuff and sleeve. Shapeless as a wet rag, it fell from his thin shoulders. The ropey line of his backbone showed from the neck. The hands, thrust out from the sagging sleeves of the sweater, were hung on wrists like dead sticks. Delore heard Walter's sarcastic voice. "Funny thing, you don't know that man. You come all this way, through that timber, all for nothing."

Mathoose half turned, rested a hand on the fir needles beside his gun and looked straight at Delore. Now he could see the side of the face that had been hidden from him. There was no ear. The jaw itself seemed drawn into the side of the face, giving it the lop-sided look of a Hallowe'en mask. All the side of the face was a sullen red in the pale light from the fire.

Mathoose was dying of cancer.

Sometime this winter, perhaps some night when the temperature was forty below and the jack pines swelled their sap and exploded like guns, when the green and the pink Northern Lights would rise and fall over his head, Mathoose would die, under trees such as these, alone, as he had been alone so many years.

Delore felt a rush of pity for the man. Whatever he had done—and who knew, was Mathoose really the murderer of those two men on the Reserve?—whatever he had done, Mathoose was in a lonely misery that few humans ever knew.

"I don't recognize your friend, Walter," said Delore.

"Sure too bad, ain't it. Seems like ain't anybody knows the Indian."

Delore turned to Walter and saw the same sardonic face—half smile, half sneer—that had been there since the beef drive left the Long Opening. What was Walter getting for this? Not money. This poor, wretched creature of the woods had none. Whisky? Walter, after all, was drinking none of it. He had waited at Sitkum Casmeer's three days, allowing foolish Anatole to soak himself in liquor while he, Walter, waited for the signal from Mathoose.

"It's a good thing when people stick together, Walter," said Delore.

Walter almost looked surprised. "You talk funny in the head, boss."

"I don't know your friend. But I think your friend needs some grub."

Walter looked at him steadily, straight in the face, not sideways from the corner of his eyes as usually.

"I think, spose you lose that extra packhorse, Walter, it won't be so bad spose that friend picks it up and takes it."

Walter's gaze never wavered. Delore glanced across at Mathoose. Mathoose fed another tiny stick to the fire.

Delore stood up. "Now I gotta go," he said. "I got one hundred and ninety-six cattle to get to Williams Lake."

Walter spoke in a voice that seemed to have all the soft music of the Indian accent peeled away from it: "I don't think you go this place yet."

"Yep," said Delore. "I got to go." He noticed from the corner of his eye that Mathoose's skeleton-thin hand was moving toward the .30-.30 and, to fill the heavy air, he kept on talking. "I ain't used to these long, long conversations, Walter."

He turned away from them. It was now too late to do anything else. As he did so he saw—he hoped he saw—that Walter's expression had passed beyond surprise and back into the mocking half-smile that was so typical of Walter Charlie. But this he would never know. Neither would he ever know if Mathoose had the .30-.30 carbine aimed between his shoulder blades as he walked away from that tiny fire in the pines.

Delore's hope was that his last remark—which he now could not remember — would be just puzzling enough to keep Mathoose's finger off the trigger until he was at the edge of the poplar grove. Then he could run and skip among the trees. He would be hard to see, if he ran zigzag through the poplar, and if a fair-sized poplar should come between him and the bullet, the bullet would probably blow up, wouldn't it? The bullets were soft-nose.

He was still only half-way to the poplar and he could feel sweat run down his chest, front and back. Would it stain his back, between his shoulder blades, and make a better target in the dim light of the fire? He walked toward the poplar at the same even pace.

It surprised even himself that when he passed the poplar he still did not run. He did not even walk faster. He just walked. After a few more yards, he said in a voice so even and calm that it amazed him, "Stella?"

The mare stirred her feet in the dry leaves ahead.

He walked to her, untied her halter, slid upon her back, walked her to the camp and never looked behind him.

When he came near the camp his knees were weak and there was a dull pain at the back of his neck, but Delore did not ride over to see Step, who would by now probably be asleep by the dim fire. Instead he saddled Stella carefully and walked her all night at the edges of the beef drive. When the dawn was near and he was walking, leading the mare in order to keep warm the thought that was strongest in his mind was that in the course of just a few days he had seen two most remarkable examples of unselfishness, and both in Indians.

There was poor stupid Anatole, who had jumped to what must have seemed certain death in the river to rescue him. And Walter. Walter who, after all, had accumulated nothing more of this world's goods than one fine sleeping bag, who had worked so hard and long to care for a dying outlaw without the faintest hope of reward or even of appreciation. What strange forces made men act as they did?

When he came back to the camp site at dawn, Step was already gone. It was only then, when he was so tired that he rolled his unzipped bag about himself while clad, boots and all, that Delore Bernard began to shake with fear for his life, which he had almost lost.

NOTHING TO DO BUT FIGHT

The sun burned hot in his face. Delore rolled over, face to the ground, and enjoyed another brief lapse into sleep, but it was very brief. It was not fair to leave so much to faithful Step-and-a-Half Jones, who must be very tired now. Delore rolled onto his back again, threw an arm across his eyes, opened them to the day, and looked at the animals of the Namko beef drive, his beef drive, now spotted across several square miles of the meadow, singly and in pairs and threes. He let his eye run up the long drift fence to where it met the timber. Some cattle, he noticed, were almost at the end of the fence, very near the end.

Delore sat up. Had some slipped around and into the open country beyond without the careful Step noticing?

The sleeping bag fell away from his shoulders. He looked across at Step's bag. Step was in it. His face, now white with heavy whiskers, showed beneath his hat that he had, sometime after sunrise, placed over his forehead to keep out the sun. Step asleep? Who was watching the drive? Perhaps Anatole had returned?

Delore threw the folds of the bag away from him.

He stood up and rubbed his hands through his short hair. Step snored.

"Step," he said.

Step did not wake.

Delore glanced quickly about the meadow, hoping to see Anatole returned to his job, walking his horse beside the fence, down at the willows by the creek, sitting perhaps on a high knoll holding his horse's reins in his hands, watching the big drive spread out over the grass below him. He looked to the slope above his camp. There, half lying by the patch of snowberry bush, was Anatole. He knew when he looked that Anatole was still drunk.

"That boss sure sleeps some late," said Anatole.

"You watching the cattle, Anatole?"

Anatole shook his head and rose, not too steadily. "I come to get something from that drive," he said.

"Where's Walter?"

Anatole paid no attention but walked, carefully placing his feet one in front of the other, toward Delore.

"I come to get something from that beef drive," he said.

"Who's riding herd?"

Anatole shook his head as though the question were a fly that bothered him. He was not smiling now.

"Sitkum Casmeer and me, we think it's good idea we get a beef to eat," he said.

"You don't kill any beef in my drive, Anatole."

"Oh." Anatole eyed him steadily. His mouth hung open a little and the stump of one old tooth came forward and touched the upper lip. "That boss he's real tough, ain't it? He says we don't get no beef to eat."

"You just forget about killing a beef. You get sobered up. We got to get this drive moving again."

Anatole again shook his head. "You don't und'stand. I get a beef from you, right now."

"You get no beef from me."

"Well," said Anatole. "So that boss acts real tough with me. Might be I beat up that boss some. Then, after I beat him up, I take that beef."

Again Delore felt cold in his legs. With a dreadful certainty he knew that this would not be like the episode at Mathoose's fire. He could do nothing but fight. No words of his would deter Anatole. Anatole had not really come to demand a beef to eat. Anatole was fighting drunk. Beef would not satisfy him. Only a fight could. The cowboy was almost a head taller than he, and perhaps thirty pounds heavier, and he remembered the toughness of this man when the blue roan had piled him, morning after morning.

"Maybe you better go back, have another drink, Anatole," said Delore.

Anatole drew open the sides of his mouth. It might be a smile or it might be a snarl but the words he next spoke left no doubt. "Might be that boss don't want to fight me."

"Go ahead. Get some more to drink. We'll wait for you."

Anatole came closer, his hands hanging by his sides.

"When I fight that boss, I guess first I cut him up some."

Delore's legs were shaking now.

Anatole continued, "Might be I really cut him up good. Might be I hurt him pretty bad, that boss."

He should shout for Step but Delore knew there was
no time. Anatole was almost on him. So he said, "All
right, I'll fight you."

Anatole stopped, surprised.

Delore continued, "But take off your jacket."

As he spoke, Delore quickly stripped off his denim
coat.

He repeated, "Take off your coat if you want a fight.
I never hit a man with his coat on."

Puzzled at first, Anatole now was almost gay.

"Sure," he said. "I take off my chacket, fight that
boss."

Anatole fumbled with his coat. He looked at Delore,
a little puzzled again. "Take off your coat he tells me,
that boss."

"I never hit a man with his coat on."

Anatole began to pull his jacket from him backward,
down both arms at the same time. When the jacket was
half-way down the arms, Delore ran three steps and hit
the cowboy squarely in the mouth. Anatole still had
a half-grin on his face when he went over backward,
the blood already spurting from his split lip. Delore ran
two more steps and drove his boots hard into Anatole's
ribs.

Anatole doubled up, knees as close to his chin as he
could pull them, face toward the ground, his hands
folded at the back of his head. The boots had been put
to him before.

Delore kicked him four times, hard, and stepped
back.

Anatole lay with his face in the dust, almost as he
had lain with his cheek on the gravel of the bar at the

Ugulkutz crossing. From his mouth blood and saliva dripped and made a small muddy pool. He rolled over on his back, looked at the sky for a moment, pulled his elbows into the ground behind him and came to a sitting position. Then he fell forward again, grunting. He placed the palms of his hands on the ground, brought up his knees beneath him and rose to a kneeling position. His dirty, bloody face looked up at Delore.

"Now you better go down the creek, get sobered up," said Delore.

Anatole got to his feet, grunted, held his hands about his belly, straightened a little and slowly, in pain, made his way toward the water.

An enemy for the rest of my life, thought Delore.

But now there was time. He would rouse Step, who had slept through all the short, bloody fight. Together he and Step could handle Anatole when he returned. Even if Anatole came back with his pistol. The pistol?

He ran to Anatole's bedroll, unused these four nights, felt beneath it, shook it, tore it away from the ground and looked beneath it. Anatole had taken his pistol.

How dangerous was a single-shot .22?

Enough to kill a man on the first shot, he knew. No matter, there was Step. Step had handled such matters before. He ran to Step's bag and shook the old cowboy's shoulder.

"Step! Wake up, Step!"

"Humppphum?" Step rolled away from him.

He shook the shoulder harder. Step grunted. He rolled Step's whiskery face back toward the sun.

"Step, I just had a fight with Anatole."

"Aha. Aha." Step seemed to be going back to sleep.

"Step. Wake up. This is important. I put the boots to Anatole. He's going to come back with his pistol. Wake up, Step."

Step snored.

"Wake up, Step. Wake up."

Delore reached down, grabbed Step by both armpits and dragged him to a sitting position. "We got trouble with Anatole. I stopped him for a minute or so, but he's going to come back with that gun he keeps in his pocket."

Step sat rocking, a small smile on his face. "An'tole's all right," he muttered.

Delore took the old cowboy's shoulders and shook them. Placing his face close to Step's, he said, "Step, this is . . ." Then he stopped. Step's breath was heavy with alcohol. He looked at Step's bleary eyes, his grin, so much like Anatole's foolish grin.

"You're drunk, man," said Delore.

"I been drunk for four days," said Step-and-a-Half Jones. "You mean you ain't noticed?"

Pulling himself from Delore's grip, Step rolled himself out of his blanket. As he did, a bottle of the colourless potato alcohol of Sitkum Casmeer rolled with him. Step grabbed it, swirled off the screw cap and drank. "I guess that shows Ol Step-and-a-Half Jones can sure hold his liquor," he said.

He stood up and fell down. The bottle rolled away, spilling its last few ounces over the grass. Step lurched after it, caught it after the last ounce had gone and looked mournfully through the neck at the dry bottom.

"Poor Step," he said. "Poor, lovable old Step-and-a-

Half Jones. Your whisky-hole is all gone dry. Well," he staggered to his feet, "it is time for more." Step lurched off toward his horse which, still saddled, had been left roped to a tree some hours before in the darkness of night.

"Step!" said Delore.

Step kept walking. He was singing to himself tunelessly, "Yes, we will gather by the river, the beyootiful, the won-der-ful ri-iver."

Delore walked beside him.

"Step," he said, "listen to me. I really need your help, Step. I really need you."

Step paused and looked toward him. He seemed to be trying either to understand what Delore had just said or to relate it to something that he vaguely remembered. Whatever his drugged mind sought, it failed to find it. He walked to his horse, untied the reins neatly, and very clumsily, almost falling off twice, managed to clamber into the high saddle.

"You gotta help me," said Delore. "Anatole is coming back with his pistol and I can't handle him. I can't handle him."

Step looked over the hill toward Sitkum's. "I just gotta get one more drink."

"Get the bottle after. Help me handle Anatole first."

Step nodded his head ponderously, as a man who has just heard a particularly wise pronouncement. "Just one more drink might do," he said. Then turning to Delore, he said, in tones of sweet reason, "Be sensible, kid. I never been able to stop in just four days."

"You can't let me down like this!"

Step kicked his heels and his patient horse walked off toward Casmeer's.

A few yards distant he stopped, turned, placed one hand on the horse's rump and spoke again to Delore. "I know, kid," he said. "I'm letting you down." He paused and seemed again to be trying to collect the thoughts of a long life of cowboying. He still did not seem to be drunk but he looked like a very, very old man. "All I can say, kid . . ." He paused to arrange his thinking again and, finally, in all the sadness of truth, added, ". . . all I can say . . . I never let you down as badly as I let myself down. All of my life."

Step turned his saddle horse to Sitkum Casmeer's and to the blackness that the old cowboy had never been able to thrust away with righteous words.

Delore ran back to the camp and hunted some more for Anatole's pistol, looking in the pack boxes, under his own sleeping bag, among the hobbles and extra bridles and the assorted harness leather, hearing his breath go harshly in and out of his dry chest as he moved. The shadow of Anatole fell across him while he pawed through the grub box. Anatole had walked up very quietly. There was no gun in Anatole's hand but his eyes seemed as bleak and murderous as before. Well, perhaps, if Anatole had no gun he could trick him again. Delore got to his feet.

The last trick would not work, of course. The man could not be fooled twice the same way. What could he do?

"That boss," said Anatole, "he's sure smart, that boss. 'Take off your coat,' he says to me, 'I don't ever hit a man has got his coat on.'"

Delore wiped his hands on his pants.

"Shmart man," said Anatole. He came two steps closer. They were now so close that their breath must be mingling in the hot air of the morning. "Smart," said Anatole. His hand moved forward.

Delore was about to jump back but, seeing the hand was open, he put his own hand out and shook Anatole's. Anatole clasped his hand firmly—a rare thing for an Indian to do because Indians' handshakes were bare touches of the palm, limp as dry cloth. Then Anatole brought his left hand over and slapped the side of Delore's, so that three hands were locked together.

"He's smart man, that boss." Anatole was really smiling. "I come up drunk. He says 'Take off your coat.'" Anatole shook his head and grinned some more.

All Delore could think to say was, "That's okay, Anatole."

A horse trotted up. It was Walter. Anatole looked over and said, "Hey. The boss on this drive, he's sure smart man. I tell you what he does . . ." Anatole loosed Delore's hand and walked over, half stooped, to Walter. Walter stepped to the ground. Anatole recounted the story in which he now seemed to take such a delight. "'Before I fight you,' that boss says, 'you take off your coat.' I take off my coat. Kapow! Kapow!" Anatole felt his ribs. "By gosh, I think might be he breaks some ribs I got, that boss."

"Better I take you down that creek," said Walter, "might be you sober up."

Anatole said, hurt, "I *been* that creek. I spend looong time in that creek." It was true. Anatole was soaking wet from head to foot. Blood still dripped from his face and he still held his hands about his chest where Delore had kicked him.

Walter took his arm. "Well, I sober you up some more," he said.

Together they started toward the lake, Anatole bent over, grunting with the pain in his ribs. Walter paused after a few steps; Anatole still faced, grunting, toward the calm waters of the little lake. Walter looked at Delore, smiled, and said as only Walter Charlie could say, "Lead, kindly light, amid the encircling gloom."

"We'll push on with the drive in an hour's time," said Delore. "You and me and Anatole. Step won't be coming in to the Lake."

"Sure," said Walter, "we're all ready one hour from now."

A couple of hours later the big drive moved out, without Step-and-a-Half Jones.

THE BROCKLEFACE

Delore had so long looked forward to the day when he would bring the Namko drive into Williams Lake that now, near the crest of the hill above the town, it surprised him that victory had so stale a taste. Perhaps it was the rain. It had sluiced down upon them all of the night before. It rained all the long day that they brought the drive down Sheep Creek Hill and over the narrow bridge on the Fraser and up through the timbered ridge, which lay between the big river and the town of Williams Lake. The cattle were nervous because they slipped on the muddy road. They looked poor. Their loins were hollow, their ribs showed, they were stupider, noisier, than he could ever remember.

Cars did stop to let the Namko drive pass, but only because the law required them to, and the slick-faced men and women and children behind the steamy windows sat, bored, listening to blaring radios, as the drive passed them. One man had rolled down his window and shouted, "Hey, kid, how long does this business last?" Delore, in spite of himself, looked down to his feet in the stirrups. Anatole had set his old riding boots too close to the fire the wet night before and they had curled up like bacon. He had thrown them into the

campfire that morning and had found himself obliged
to wear black-and-white running shoes this day. These,
like all his clothes, were soaked and clung to his bones.
He saw that his jeans were torn at the knee and also
noticed that behind his knee bones the flesh of his legs
caved in toward the thigh bones.

"Beef drive," he said, and walked Stella past the car.

When they came down the twisting road into
Williams Lake, the town was grey and flat beneath
them and there were no newspaper reporters or anyone else to meet them at the Holding Ground.

Delore was counting the last few of the one hundred
and ninety-six squelching past the Holding Ground
gate when his father came up in a late-model station
wagon. A middle-aged man in a neat suit and a forty-
dollar Stetson drove the wagon. Delore judged him to
be a buyer. Frenchie got out of the wagon wearing the
same clothes that he had worn the morning that he fell
beneath the Green Mountain Morgan, except that one
leg was encased in a dirty, mud-spattered plaster cast.
His big toes poked out the open end of the cast. On
the other leg he wore his one remaining good riding
boot but it, too, was now caked in old and new mud.
He was using crutches.

Delore did not turn his head when he heard the two
men come out the doors of the station wagon. He continued to count cattle as they went past him at the gate
of the Holding Ground. He heard the buyer say,
"Quite a thing, Frenchie, when you got a son old
enough to boss the Namko drive," but he could not
hear his father answer.

Frenchie and the buyer came up beside him at the gate. He looked and saw that his father was counting heads inside the Holding Ground, his eyes blocking out the shifting red and brown herd three by three, totalling them with the lightning speed that never ceased to be amazing.

To the right of his mare the buyer said, "You're Young Frenchie?"

"Delore Bernard," he said.

"It's a pleasure to meet you," the man said, and reached up to shake his hand. "You get them all in?"

"The Ugulkutz boomed up," Delore said. "We had to swim it." He thought back on the long twenty-four days and said, "I guess that was all that was interesting."

"Apart from that," said the buyer, "nothing to report." He was a heavy man and his belly hung over the Mexican silver buckle on his belt. Delore liked the way he smiled.

"Nothing to report," said Delore.

The buyer laughed and repeated, "Nothing to report," and turning to Frenchie said, more loudly, "Sounds familiar, eh, Frenchie? Nothing unusual."

But Frenchie broke in upon him almost before the words were in the air. "Look hat dat!" said Frenchie. He pounded his fist upon the rail beside the gate and repeated, "Look hat dat!"

His thin, sharp nose was turned toward the old brockleface cow at the far end of the herd. Stringy and stupid as she was, she had come all the way with the Namko drive. Frenchie slapped the fence rail again. "He beat you. Stetler beat you out of a good steer."

Delore said, "I never noticed until we were away from his place."

"He beat you," said Frenchie. He stared at Delore. "What was the last thing I told you? What did I last say in that meadow?"

When Delore did not answer Frenchie continued, "I said . . ."—he pounded the rail some more—"I said that brockleface is for Stetler. I said, 'Watch Stetler. Make sure he don't take a good steer.'"

Delore looked first at his father, then at the buyer. The buyer winked. He seemed amused.

Frenchie turned his leathery face toward Delore and his eyes were like two small black diamonds. "He beat you. Stetler beat you."

"Nothing unusual," said the buyer.

Frenchie looked at the buyer, rubbed his right wrist on the sharp point of his nose and said, "Aaaakh." Then he turned his head toward the Namko drive in the Holding Ground, counted it again and, turning to the buyer, said, "Kids! Kids!" He looked straight at Delore. "Ah, well," said Frenchie, "I guess you'll learn, spose you live long henough."

Frenchie said no more, but the buyer was smiling when he reached up and shook Delore's hand and called him "Mr. Bernard," and when Anatole Harry and Walter Charlie came up to him they called him "Boss" and shook hands with the right hand and laid the left hand over his knuckles, and as Delore rode down to town through the mud, with the water squelching through the canvas of his running shoes, he felt that, all things considered, he hadn't done too bad a job.